HARLEM MOON ✳ BROADWAY

Drama
Is Her Middle Name

WENDY WILLIAMS

and

KAREN HUNTER

☆ ★ ☆ THE RITZ HARPER CHRONICLES, VOL. 1 ★

PUBLISHED BY HARLEM MOON

Copyright © 2006 by Wendy Williams and Karen Hunter

All Rights Reserved

Published in the United States by Harlem Moon, an imprint of The Doubleday
Broadway Publishing Group, a division of Random House, Inc., New York.

HARLEM MOON, BROADWAY BOOKS, and the HARLEM MOON logo, depicting a moon
and a woman, are trademarks of Random House, Inc. The figure in the Harlem
Moon logo is inspired by a graphic design by Aaron Douglas (1899–1979).

Cataloging-in-Publication Data is on file with the Library of Congress

ISBN-13: 978-0-7394-7004-6

PRINTED IN THE UNITED STATES OF AMERICA

To every woman who's doing it for herself—making her own money, taking care of her health, holding down her position at home and at work (without tears).

Sisters, we are doing it for ourselves!

Acknowledgments

I am going to keep this simple. I want to thank my husband, Kevin, and my son, Kevin, who give me a reason to keep doing what I'm doing. To my mother, father, sister, and brother, who are always there for me, I love you very much.

Thanks to Steve Lindsey, who keeps me fab-u-lous!

Thanks to my very competent and wonderful writing partner and friend, Karen Hunter.

Thanks to everyone at Harlem Moon/Broadway for believing in Ritz Harper and making it happen.

And last but not least, I want to thank my radio fans for staying with me this long and for embracing my fertile imagination. I love you all for listening . . . and now reading!

Drama

Is Her Middle Name

☆ ★ ☆

_1_

"I love you for listening!" Ritz signed off the air as she did every evening. She quickly scooped up the papers she had scattered on the desk in front of her and stuffed them into her white crocodile Gucci bag.

"Um, Ritz, you have a couple of faxes here that I think you should look at," said Jamie, nervously handing the papers over to Ritz. Jamie was the newest intern in a string to work on the _Ritz Harper Excursion_—one of the most popular radio shows in the country, syndicated from flagship station WHOT in New York City. Jamie had outlasted the ten before her by a month and counting.

"Do you want me to pick up your clothes from the cleaners?" she asked.

"Thanks, I'll get them myself. I have some time to kill and the fresh air will do me some good. Chas, are you coming?"

"Uh-uh. I have to clean up some of the mess you made today, Miss Thing," he said with his usual hint of attitude and humor. "But wait up, I'll walk you downstairs."

Jamie left to prepare for the next day's show. Chas grabbed his mink-lined shearling and Ritz slung her white fur over her slim frame. Winter white, head to toe. It was a typical Ritz outfit. If she didn't have a fly fur or some other extravagant accessory, she simply was not dressed.

She and Chas waited at the bank of elevators and rode the thirty-nine floors down to the lobby without stopping, like an express train. At this time of night, there were very few people left in the building.

At the lobby level, Ritz let her four-inch Jimmy Choos clop on the marble floor. She loved the sound heels made on marble, like a regal Clydesdale on a cobblestone road. She also loved the way stylish heels made her feel. Ritz, who had big doe eyes, dark sumptuous Godiva chocolate skin, a chiseled jaw, and Robin Givens-esque dimples, didn't always look or feel stylish. She just started wearing heels regularly a few years back—thanks to Chas—but had mastered them to the point where she could practically run a forty-yard dash in anything under five inches.

"So what do you and Tray-Tray have planned for tonight?" Chas asked.

"Nothing special, just some girl talk," Ritz said. "We have a lot of catching up to do. It's been almost a year."

"I know! Homegirl just packed up and never looked back,"

Chas said. "I miss her. She would have enjoyed the past few months of this ride, chile."

"I know. I know," Ritz said. "I'm just glad she's here for the next event. I'm a little nervous about my first real television gig. With her behind-the-scenes knowledge, she'll be a huge help."

"Don't worry about a thing, Ritzy! Papa Chas has it all worked out," he said, glancing at his watch as Ritz headed for the revolving doors. Chas, whose given name was Charles Bradley and would never be known as Chuck or Charlie, always took care of things for Ritz.

"Give Tracee a huge sloppy kiss for me on the lips!"

Ritz shot Chas a look. "Now you went too far with that one."

"Can't blame a brother for trying!" he said and playfully pushed her toward the door.

"Bye! I'll call you later."

"Be safe, sweetie."

THIRTY-SIXTH STREET AND MADISON AVENUE, MANHATTAN

Ritz Harper checked her frosty Franck Muller watch. It was eight minutes past seven. She had some time to kill before picking up her best friend, Tracee, at the airport. It was a crisp thirty degrees. Ritz loved the winter because it gave her a chance to luxuriate in the many kinds of furs—from chin-chilla to mink, fox to ermine.

She decided to take the scenic route to her car and stop by the cleaners before heading to Newark Airport. By then, rush-hour traffic through Midtown and along the New Jersey Turnpike would be clear.

New York City, usually known for its bustle—the city that never sleeps—had a few pockets that were completely dead. After Ritz left her studio on Thirty-fourth and Park, street traffic amounted to just a few passersby. There wasn't the usual horn-blowing, anxious-to-get-nowhere car traffic that was found on the far West or East Side of town.

The Morgan Library stood out on the north side of Thirty-sixth. Its awesome white stone structure—barren, abandoned for nearly four years—was a couple of years from re-opening. There were metal and wood scaffolds and orange construc-tion barricades surrounding it. The construction crew cleared out a little after five-thirty. The apartment buildings across the street seemed like mini abandoned museums themselves. Many of the residents were either in for the night or out par-tying. The street was quiet. The only illumination came from a dull streetlight near Park Avenue on Thirty-sixth.

Ritz loved this neighborhood. Ever since she began work-ing in the city five years ago, she imagined living on the Upper East Side and on nice days walking down Park Avenue before her shift, catching lunch at the Four Seasons, even shopping at the expensive stores and of course, being hounded by adoring fans wanting her autograph. It was a fantasy that

Ritz had had since she was a little girl. It was a fantasy that she was now living out. But the reality didn't quite live up to the fantasy. Ritz didn't realize how much she loved her privacy and how shocked she would be to have people come up to her while she was eating or strolling the streets and ask for an autograph. Some were much more rude than she could have imagined, but for the most part, Ritz enjoyed the fame. She loved connecting with her people—who in some ways had become her family.

By the time Ritz left the glass and steel building that housed her studio and headed northwest toward the cleaners, about a dozen people stopped to speak, wave, or get an autograph.

"Heyyyyy, Ritz!" a very loud young woman squealed from across Park Avenue, jarring Ritz out of her thoughts. Ritz was growing to understand that her relationship with her audience was so intimate that people felt totally comfortable with her—as if they really knew her.

A portly woman in her mid-forties yelled out, "Ritz, you go! I listen everyday!" Ritz smiled and waved. On her walk up Thirty-fifth toward Madison, a woman in her early twenties, who was walking with two friends, asked for an autograph. "Sorry, sweetie, no time," Ritz said. "I have to run. But I love ya!" Ritz picked up her pace as she passed the Community Church of New York.

For every block and wave and hello, a beige Nissan followed Ritz.

A couple more fans greeted her and someone in a black Jeep Cherokee beeped his horn and yelled out, "Will you marry me?!" as he made a right onto Madison, past Ritz, who gave a bright smile.

"I imagined this," she said to herself remembering the fantasies of adoring fans, autograph hounds, and paparazzi. "But I never imagined *this*." For four years Ritz had languished in abject obscurity on WHOT doing nights. She was good, that's why she kept her position. But she wasn't quite good enough to break out. One night Ritz did something different, and it changed her life. This was the night her fate shifted— her career literally exploded. She and her camp referred to it as "the Bomb Drop." The Bomb Drop also disintegrated the career of the nation's most respected and famous newswoman and changed the face not just of Ritz's career but of radio itself. The gloves came off and everyone became fair game. Stations like WHOT, which previously were committed to playing the hottest music in the country, started looking for "personalities" instead of "announcers." They wanted jocks like Ritz who could be bigger than the music. Ritz was an "overnight" sensation—four years in the making.

"This ain't no fifteen minutes of fame, baby," she would say. "This is for keeps!"

That's why she enjoyed the days that she drove into the city—which were becoming fewer and fewer. Usually the station would send a car to pick up or drop Ritz off. She had so many appearances to make during the week that they didn't want her to worry about catching a cab. She was treated like a queen. But some of the perks kept her from the thing she enjoyed most—interacting with *her* people.

Ritz was rarely alone anymore. Chas—her producer and the mastermind who turned her into a real diva and took her radio game to the next level—usually escorted her to her car after the show. He parked in the same garage, and during their "wind-down" walk, they would discuss the day's show and plan for the next day.

The February air was crisp and cold. Ritz pulled her white, calf-length mink tighter. She was known for her furs. She had even rocked a midriff fox in the dead of summer for an MTV Award red carpet. Ritz adjusted her Gucci frames carefully, keeping her weave in place. Sun or no sun, Ritz always had her frames on. She liked her new look, which Chas had urged her to make. She was about twenty pounds thinner, and had new hair and a new attitude. She even bought a brand-new Aston Martin V12 Vanquish—a gift to herself with her first bonus check for coming in first place in the afternoon drive time in the last Arbitron ratings book. Chas had finally convinced the once-frugal Ritz that if she was going to be a star, she had to have the "tricks of the trade."

"You have to look like a star and live like a star," Chas told her. "You have to have star shit!"

Ritz's first thought after adding the car, one of the final pieces to her reconstruction, was "Wait until Tracee sees me!" Tracee was not only Ritz's best friend, she was the one person who was truly happy about Ritz's success. There was no jealousy, no cattiness, no phoniness with Tracee—just sheer friendship and sheer joy. That was a rarity for Ritz, who had very few female friends—and very few friends, period.

"She is going to fall out when she sees this Vanquish!" said Ritz, who was with Tracee when she bought her Lexus convertible two years before. The two of them drove around Manhattan with the top down, heat blasting. It was last year this time. They were shivering and screaming with laughter the whole time. Ritz had so much to share with Tracee, who seemed so distant lately—and it had nothing to do with the twelve hundred–plus miles she'd moved away. So much had changed. Ritz had changed, too.

Ritz smiled and tingled with excitement thinking about reconnecting with her friend. She was so caught up in her own thoughts that she never noticed the beige Nissan that was still trailing her. Ritz didn't see the Nissan slow down as she stopped for the light, crossing the street between Thirty-fifth and Thirty-sixth. She didn't spot it as it waited midblock while Ritz ran into the cleaners on Thirty-sixth and Madison. Her only reason for taking this route was to make sure her pink gown was ready. She was making her debut on Monday on her very own red carpet, hosting the Grammys for E! She'd had to have the dress taken in to make sure it fit like a snake's skin. She couldn't wait to get Tracee's feedback on the dress. And if didn't fit, she had all day Saturday to find an emergency tailor to fix it.

Ritz was mentally going over her checklist of things to do. She even had activities mapped out for Tracee even though Tracee hated planned activities. There would be a day at the spa at the Hilton in Short Hills. Ritz could afford the Ritz, the Peninsula, Bliss, or any upscale spa, but she wanted to stay close to home. The Hilton also held special memories for Ritz and Tracee. Before Tracee moved, the two would meet there at least once a month for a massage.

"You have to take care of yourself," Tracee would say. "You have to beat all of that stress out of your body."

The Hilton in Short Hills was affordable and close to Ritz's home. Traipsing off to New York on the weekend would be counterproductive to the stress relief she was seeking. Tracee would usually stay over, and they would either watch a DVD and eat popcorn or plot their next move. The two shared their dreams—Ritz of taking over radio and Tracee of taking over the music business.

Two years later, Ritz had fulfilled most of her dreams, and Tracee had done a one-eighty from hers.

It was during one of their girls-out weekends when Tracee confided in Ritz that she was tired of the hustle.

"I just believe God has other plans for me, Ritzy," she would say. "I feel like every day I stay in this game, I am losing part of my soul. I just feel it draining away, like it's being siphoned off. I can't do it anymore."

One month later she was packing up and moving off to Florida.

"Damn, girl, you could have at least moved to South Beach or some fly-ass place like that," Ritz said. "Ain't nobody in Winter Garden but some old-ass retired people who can't drive. What the fuck?"

"That's exactly what I wanted—minus the bad driving," Tracee said. "Peace and quiet."

Ritz missed her friend. She spent five hours a day, five days a week, talking to millions over the airwaves. But talking to Tracee was something that nothing could replace. She couldn't wait to wear her out at her favorite mall—The Mall at Short Hills, directly across the street from the Hilton spa. She could finally let her hair down and tell someone how scared she was at everything that was happening to her.

Ritz had developed an on-air style that titillated, thrilled, and pissed people off all at the same time. And it was contagious. Even those who hated her—and the list was growing—could not turn the dial when she was on. It had been less than six months since she debuted in the afternoon drive spot on WHOT, but Ritz's audience and her salary had tripled. Ritz Harper was the undisputed queen of the radio.

Privately, Ritz was quite different—not at all confident and self-assured. Some nights, after hosting a sold-out party or being seen on television in an interview, Ritz would go home to a beautiful, huge home with all the amenities, put on her flannel pajamas, curl into a ball, and cry. Despite everything she had, she felt very alone, and was very lonely. The irony of talking for a living was that Ritz didn't really have anyone to talk to. Chas was cool and he was like having a close girlfriend. But he wasn't. Tracee was the only one who really understood—who had been there before Ritz was *the* Ritz Harper. When she was simply Ritgina (a combination of the name of her father, Ritchie, whom she never knew, and her mother, Gina) Harper.

As Ritz crossed Madison Avenue heading toward the garage near Park, she pulled her white Gucci sack tighter over her shoulder, checked her watch again, and picked up her pace. So did the Nissan. She could see the nose of her V12 Vanquish in the entrance of the garage. Ritz loved Ramon for always having her car ready for her, no matter how late she came down from the studio. She hated to wait. It was almost seven-twenty, and she had an hour to get to Newark.

"Oh, shoot!" Ritz said to herself. "I better hurry the hell up."

She broke into a light trot. The Nissan pulled up beside her, the power window rolling down on the passenger side facing Ritz. She slowed down, thinking the car was another fan. The windows of the car were tinted. It was New York, and these days just about everyone had a tint darker than the law allowed.

"Ritz Harper?" a gravelly voice spoke out.

In an instant, Ritz saw a flash of light from the window and felt a burning sensation in her chest. She started to run. She looked around in a panic, and there was no one in sight. "Where the fuck are all the people?" she thought. Ritz wanted to scream but nothing would come out.

"Just keep running!" she thought.

The garage was about a hundred feet away.

"I can make it," she said silently to herself.

The car sped up and from the open passenger window Ritz caught more flashes from her peripheral vision. The burning, searing heat Ritz felt in her side and in her shoulder was now pulsating. The Nissan's window went up slowly and the car gradually picked up speed as the driver headed north, blending perfectly into the Midtown Tunnel traffic.

Still clutching her bag, Ritz fell hard to her knees, then collapsed on her side and finally rolled onto her back and let out a faint gasp. Her Gucci frames fell to the ground.

Up the street, a young Asian man stepped outside to smoke a cigarette. He looked down the block a bit, squinted, and noticed something that looked like a dog lying on the ground. All he could make out from that distance was the animal's fur. As he got closer, he began frantically patting himself down in search of his cell phone.

A few more people started toward the object on the sidewalk, noticing the bloodstains on the concrete and the figure on the ground.

"I think that's Ritz Harper!" a twentyish man said to his friend. "That's fucking Ritz Harper! Oh, shit!"

The friend, a young girl, looked around and bent down next to Ritz and slyly picked up her Gucci frames, slipping them into the pocket of her leather jacket.

A crowd began to form.

As Ritz lay on the ground, she could hear faint voices. People using camera phones began taking pictures. Ritz was numb. She couldn't move. She was too angry to think about death. Her anger had so much power that it kept her heart pumping even when her vital signs were fading. She heard sirens in the distance. Ritz felt like she was floating above her own body. She was in and out, but one thought kept pounding through, replaying like a skipped record: "Who the fuck did this to me?! Who the fuck did this?! Who the fuck . . . ?!"

Ritgina Harper was a little annoyed when the principal called her to the office over the loudspeaker during Mrs. Johnson's second-period class at George W. Carver Elementary School in downtown Richmond, Virginia. Ritgina loved school and she particularly loved Mrs. Johnson's class. She made her students do things like watch *Roots* and write a paper on how the miniseries changed their views, and she had them memorize every capital of all fifty states.

Mrs. Johnson was having a competition that morning. The student who could get the most state capitals correct would win a special prize. Ritgina wanted the prize—she didn't care what it was. She just loved to win. Her mother, Gina, had stayed up late last night quizzing her.

"Come on, Ritz! You know Mommy has to get up early in the morning," her mother complained after going through all fifty for the eighth time. "You are going to do fine, I just know it."

"Mommy, just one more time, please, please, please!" Ritgina said. "I'll give you extra kisses and I'll get up extra early and make your coffee for you."

"You sure drive a hard bargain, young lady," her mother said, rubbing her weary eyes. "Okay, okay. What is the capital of Alaska?"

"Anchorage! That one was easy, Mommy. Give me a hard one."

"How about South Dakota?" A minute passed. "Ah-ha! I stumped you. It's Pierre. Write it down and study it. I'll grill you some more after you make my coffee in the morning. Now take your little tail to bed."

Ritz kissed her mother good night, and grabbed her notebook, in which she wrote Pierre, South Dakota; Montpelier, Vermont; and Concord, New Hampshire—the three states that stumped her, which she had to master by the morning. And master them she would.

"I love you, Mommy!"

"I love *you*, my beautiful young lady!"

Gina doted on her daughter. It was just the two of them since Ritgina was a baby. Ritchie didn't stick around but a week after Ritgina was born, leaving the eighteen-year-old Gina to fend for herself and her baby. Gina hated Ritchie for that and didn't want to be reminded of him. So she started calling her little girl Ritz. As early as she could, Gina started filling Ritz's head with survival skills.

Around the age of nine, Ritz's mother started talking to her about adult issues: "Don't let no man take advantage of you, sweet talking you to try and get funny with you! I haven't met a man yet who wasn't up to no good."

"Maaaaaa!" Ritz would protest. "Nobody's even thinking about all of that."

"You'd be surprised, young lady, what these men are thinking about," her mother would say. "I don't want you ever to be dependent on no man for nothing. You are going to use that brain of yours, get an education, and take care of yourself. And maybe you'll even make enough money to take care of your old mother one day."

"You are a smart little girl," her mother said on another occasion. "But if you want to be the best, you have to work hard—outwork everyone. Hard work is what separates the good from the best. And you will be the best!"

Gina led by example. She never finished high school, but she always worked at least two jobs. She refused to be a statistic. She was a single mother, but she wasn't going to be a poor single mother on welfare whose children grow up to follow in her footsteps. For one, she was determined to make sure that Ritgina would be an only child. It was hard enough taking care of one child; she was not going to have any more. To make sure, Gina didn't date. There would never be a man to come in between her and her daughter. There would never be any threat to break that bond. She had plans for her baby girl, and those plans started with a solid education. Gina started saving early for Ritgina's college education, even though she knew her little girl would qualify for a scholarship. Just in case, though, Gina would make sure she had not only enough for school, but for books and any other incidentals her child would need.

With every paycheck, Gina bought a savings bond. It wasn't much but she had been doing that since Ritgina was a baby and had more than ten thousand dollars in saving bonds—not including interest.

Gina was determined to have the best of everything for herself and her daughter. Her day job as a café waitress started at six-thirty in the morning. She finished work there at two in the afternoon, giving her enough time to meet Ritz at school and walk her home, help her with her homework, cook dinner, and get her ready for the next day. She had an evening job from seven until ten, cleaning offices. During those hours Ritz was a latchkey kid. She was mature enough to take care of herself for about three hours, and she knew the rules: "Don't answer the phone or the door for nothing!" Gina and Ritz had a special code. Gina would let the phone ring once, hang up, and then call back. Then and only then was Ritz to answer the phone.

Ritz spent the three hours reading. She loved to read— everything from Judy Bloom to V. C. Andrews. She also loved mythology.

By the time Ritz's mother dragged herself into their tiny three-room apartment around ten-thirty, Ritz would usually be asleep. Gina would never turn in herself until she grabbed her little girl and gave her a big hug and a sloppy kiss on her pudgy, dimpled cheek. Gina loved her little girl's dimples and her smooth, perfect chocolaty complexion.

"She looks so much like her father," she thought. "Damn him! He is missing the best part of himself—the best thing he has ever done."

"You know Mommy loves you, don't you?"

"Yes, Mommy," Ritz would say. "I love you, too."

☆ ★ ☆

Ritgina Harper, please come to the principal's office immediately!

"Oooooh!" a chorus rang out among her classmates. Ritz Harper was apparently in big trouble.

A puzzled look crossed Ritz's face. She was mischievous and loved to play practical jokes, but never during school hours. In school she was all-business and was never in trouble.

She collected her books and put them in her book bag, then shot another puzzled look at Mrs. Johnson, who was preparing the class for the contest.

"Don't worry, Ritgina, you will have a chance at the prize when you come back," said Mrs. Johnson, not knowing why the principal wanted Ritz but couldn't imagine it was anything to worry about. "Okay, class, settled down. Let's have a practice round. Let's start from the beginning. What is the capital of Alabama?"

Ritz walked out of the classroom, down the long corridor,

and headed to the left, to the west end of the building where the principal's office was. She kept trying to think "What did I do? What could I have done?" She kept coming up blank. But as soon as she entered the office, she knew it was something really bad.

Her aunt Madalyn was there with reddened, swollen eyes. Her bottom lip began to tremble as she grabbed Ritz in a tight hug and started crying uncontrollably. Trying to collect herself, Aunt Madalyn finally managed to speak. "Sweetie . . . there has been a terrible, terrible accident. Your—your mother . . . your mother is . . . she's gone." Aunt Madalyn lost it.

Aunt Madalyn's words didn't register immediately. Gone? Gone where?

Gina had used her thirty-minute break from the café at ten A.M. to rush a couple of blocks to the local bookstore. She wanted to surprise Ritz with the next V. C. Andrews book as a reward for the hard work she had been doing in school. On her way back to work, Gina ran in the middle of the street. A Budweiser beer truck came whipping around the corner at the same time. The impact was so horrific that witnesses hoped that her heart stopped immediately. Gina was, however, alive for an hour after the accident, but she never regained consciousness.

The funeral and the weeks that followed were a blur for Ritz. She was eleven years old and had lost her best friend, her biggest champion. She loved Aunt Madalyn and her husband of twenty-two years, Uncle Cecil. But they weren't a substitute for her mother. Her mother was still vibrant and young. Uncle Cecil and Aunt Madalyn were only in their mid-forties, but they were raised in a time when forty was more like sixty. Aunt Madalyn was fifteen years older than her sister Gina. She was more like a great-aunt. And she had old-fashioned ways, which in the long run benefited Ritz by refining her. But a girl of eleven didn't appreciate that refining process. On one of her few days off, it wasn't unusual for Gina to take Ritz to a water park or on a picnic. Aunt Madalyn would take her to the theater. Her mom was young and hip and didn't mind Ritz dressing like a kid. Gina sometimes dressed like a kid herself. Aunt Madalyn had Ritz dressing like a "lady"—an *old* lady. But even though Ritz didn't realize it until later, living with Aunt Madalyn and Uncle Cecil was one of the best things to happen to her.

Ritz got to see that all men weren't really that bad, as her mother had led her to believe they were. Uncle Cecil was not only one of the nicest people Ritz had ever met, he absolutely adored Aunt Madalyn and said all the time that he was "tickled pink" to have a daughter, because he and Aunt Madalyn couldn't have kids. Ritz never knew whose "fault" it was, but she did know that living there, she was treated like a porcelain doll, a little princess. While her mother worked hard to give her little things, it seemed like Uncle Cecil and Aunt Madalyn always had money for big things. Aunt Madalyn didn't work. Uncle Cecil owned a contracting company and while he kept long hours, he always had a pocket full of cash. When he got home, he would take his ladies out for ice cream after dinner. Aunt Madalyn always had dinner ready for him when he came home. To Ritz, it seemed that Aunt Madalyn and Uncle Cecil were a throwback to those 1950s shows like *Leave It to Beaver*, except they were dipped in sepia.

3

Ritz punched the alarm code to her Jersey City apartment, set her keys on the tiny, marble-top table at the front door, sat in her comfortable, chenille-covered chair, and grabbed the remote and the unfinished Black & Mild blunt from her Orrefors ashtray. This was her routine. Ritz loved routine and order because so much of her life had been chaos, beyond her control. From the death of her mother to the crazy course of her career—there was so much that Ritz could simply not control that the things she could control, she controlled to the extreme.

Smoking a blunt gave her a strange sense of control and power. It was her secret rebellion—a breaking away of always doing the right thing. It was also something she did that no one—virtually no one—knew.

"Girl, you are already crazy, the last thing you need is some weed on top of all of that!" Tracee had said, the first time she saw Ritz roll a blunt. The two had been hanging out for a year, but it was the first time Ritz really let her hair down in front of Tracee.

"This is what keeps me from being completely crazy," Ritz said. "Here, you should try it. It might loosen your tight ass up, Miss Prude."

"Everybody I know smokes. It's the one thing that sets me apart," Tracee said. "It was the one thing I *thought* we had in common."

"So are you going to stop liking me now?" Ritz asked as she took a long pull on her blunt and blew a thin smoky stream into the air.

"Who said I liked you?"

The two fell back on the couch and giggled and ate. Tracee didn't need the munchies to enjoy eating. And Ritz didn't need her blunt to know that Tracee was the best friend she had ever had. In both radio and the music business there were few mentors for women. Every successful woman looked at newcomers as competition, potential threats to their position. It was next to impossible to have a female friend to trust in those businesses. Ritz was happy she had Tracee and vice versa.

Ritz took another toke of her blunt. Pangs of loneliness were starting to set in. The smoke was quickly absorbed into her Ionic Breeze air filter.

Why did she have to move all the way the fuck to Florida?

Daydreaming about missing her friend had become part of her routine. It had been about a year since Tracee had moved. And Ritz was realizing how empty her life was. The weed and the daily grind of the station provided some comfort, filled in some of the spaces. But . . .

Girl, you need a change. You need a real change.

Ritz's routine was too routine. Her show was nearly perfect. Her intros, flawless. She read commercials better than most. She was a great interviewer. She even handled her outrageous callers with aplomb. Ritz was a pro. A pro's pro. But for some reason, she still wasn't satisfied. It didn't seem to be good enough.

She had been doing her night shift for four years. For four years her time checks had been perfect. Her intros were perfect. She was perfect. But her show wasn't spectacular. It didn't stand out. Ritz wanted to stand out. She didn't want to be just another jock.

She dozed off in her comfortable, oversized chair, waking up to reruns of the *Honeymooners* at three in the morning. She dragged herself to bed, thinking about what she needed to do to distinguish herself, to get into a drive-time slot. The phone woke her up at nine on the dot, as it had every day since she moved to New Jersey.

"Hey, Auntie M," Ritz said, sounding as if she had been up for hours. She liked calling her Aunt Madalyn "Auntie M" because it reminded her of the *Wizard of Oz*. Ritz had always felt connected to that story of a little girl with no parents, raised by an aunt. Ritz felt she had a lot in common with Dorothy, including an Auntie Em.

Ritz always looked forward to the call that came every morning at nine, a wake-up call that Ritz had grown to depend on. No matter what time Ritz got in—some nights if she had an appearance, it would be nearing four when she got home—her aunt would call at nine. Aunt Madalyn's call jump-started Ritz's day and got her off on the right foot. It was almost a superstition. Aunt Madalyn, who listened to Ritz online on the computer Ritz set up for her and Uncle Cecil, would critique Ritz's show from the night before, and Ritz loved getting the reviews.

"That was a nice first hour, sweetie," Aunt Madalyn would say.

"Tell the truth! You only heard the first hour."

"You know me too well, baby. I fell asleep. Your uncle Cecil had me rubbing his back, and I got so tired I just shut down the computer and went to bed."

"I bet you did! You fell asleep? Sure. I know y'all got your freak on!"

"Ritz!"

Ritz loved embarrassing her aunt, who was always so prim and proper.

In the three years since Ritz took over the night shift on WHOT, her aunt called every day to encourage her, to give her advice, and to just be an ear for Ritz to sound off to.

"Auntie M, I don't know why I'm stuck on this night shift."

"Don't you worry," said Aunt Madalyn. "It's just a matter of time. God is just preparing you—making you sit in the sauce until you're ready. Just be patient. You always want everything yesterday, but a beautiful flower takes time to root."

"I know I'm better than everyone on my station, Auntie M. My program director keeps telling me how much he loves my work ethic and my delivery and all of that, but three years on nights is getting real tired."

Ritz's career was building. When she got the shift four years ago, there wasn't a happier person. How many jocks just a couple of years out of college land in New York City—the Big Freaking Apple? Media capital of the world! She was most proud that she didn't have to start on overnights—midnight until five in the morning. Most rookies started on overnights. It was more of a tryout spot. You either got bumped into a better shift or bumped off altogether. Some people got stuck on overnights, usually those who either had marginal talent but rarely made mistakes or those who were perfectly suited for overnights—a rare find.

Ritz started on the evening shift—six to ten, which followed the coveted afternoon drive shift. Drive time was close enough for Ritz to smell. After about two and a half years, that smell turned into a stench. She watched her station fire one sorry afternoon jock after another and never once look her way. They brought in Dr. Mark, a best-selling author whose specialty was sex. He was a cross between Dr. Ruth and

Dr. Phil with a little Dr. Strangelove thrown in for good measure. He had a devilish wit and a nasty sense of humor that would make R. Kelly blush.

His show had taken off with female callers wanting to know how to find a good man. He had capitalized on the trend of lonely women, which was only getting worse. Women didn't know where to turn for a good man.

There was "on the down low," and JL King and gay men pretending to be straight. There was the rash of "good men" with good jobs and professions marrying Asian and white women, leaving the "sisters" in the lurch. There were already five women for every man in most major cities, and those numbers were far worse in the black community. Tyler Perry made a mint doing plays and movies like *Diary of a Mad Black Woman* that basically celebrated the plight of women dealing with low-down-dirty dogs. There were enough of those women to keep a show going indefinitely. Dr. Mark had more than enough material, and he was becoming very popular because women viewed him as their savior. He had all of the answers—or at least enough to keep them calling in for advice. WHOT saw big numbers. Ritz saw red.

She called a meeting with her program director, Ernest Ruffin, whom everyone called Ruff. "Ruff, I don't get a shot at the afternoon drive?! Not even a chance?"

"Come on, Ritz. You're not ready," Ruff said. "Next to morning drive, this is our biggest moneymaking shift. Dr. Mark comes with a new audience that we need to reach, and sponsors love his success in publishing."

"I understand the business!" Ritz shot back. "Look at the numbers, Ruff. I have quite a following, too."

Ritz was No. 3 in the evening in New York. It was nothing to sneeze at. She had a loyal following that was more than a million strong.

"But Dr. Mark has a *national* audience, and we're looking at syndication," Ruff said. "Ritz, you know we love you here. I believe in you. But business is business. You'll get your turn, just be patient."

Ruff reached out and pulled Ritz close to him to give her a hug. It was an uncomfortable moment that could have turned sexual quite easily if Ritz allowed it. She knew that Ruff had a slight crush on her but she never fed it. She'd watched too many women make it to the top of their field by being on top of their boss, grinding him into submission. But Ritz wanted to make it on her own merits and on-air talent.

After a couple of minutes, Ritz pried herself away from Ruff's clutches just before he tried to snuggle his face into her neck.

"Yes, I'll get my turn. You just better hope it's here, Ruff. Because if someone else gives me a shot at the afternoon drive in this town, you'll be very sorry you ever hired this Dr. Doolittle or whatever his name is."

"Now, now, Ritz. Don't be catty. We're a team here. We all have to play to win. I'll make sure you're well taken care of."

Ritz was not convinced. The next day her aunt called as usual. Before Aunt Madalyn could get a good "How are you doing?" out, Ritz was already ranting.

"Amateurs! Amateurs! They have these people who have never done radio sitting in the big seats, the money seats. While I, who studied, went to school for this stuff, paid my dues, get passed over. It's not fair!"

Calmly, Aunt Madalyn listened—as she did when Ritz was a little girl and would come home with a gripe about a teacher giving her an A-minus instead of the A-plus she thought she deserved. She waited for Ritz to finish, then said, "No, sweetie, it's not fair. But you cannot stop doing what you're doing. Your time will come, trust me."

"That's the same thing Ruff told me," said Ritz. "But when? When?!"

"That I can't tell you. But water seeks its own level, and cream always rises to the top."

"It seems like my cream is curdling. It's getting boring every night. The same old songs, the same old promos, the same old words. I feel like I'm not getting better. Maybe I should go to another market. Maybe Philadelphia or Detroit?"

"You're in the best place you can possibly be," Aunt Madalyn tried to reason. "People would kill to be where you are, honey. Everybody is trying to get to New York. You're already there. You better not give up that seat. Have some patience."

"Auntie M, that patience stuff if wearing thin," Ritz said. "You don't understand."

"I understand better than you think. Don't lose yourself in your frustrations, baby. Stay focused on being the best you can be and it'll pay off."

Ritz's frustrations were getting the better of her. Every night when she got home, she would stay up a couple of hours watching reruns of the newsmagazine shows. There seemed to be a revolving door of "fresh" faces covering the entertainment scene but very little talent.

"Whatever happened to people working their way to the top?" Ritz asked herself as she watched that Latin chick who once was a fill-in get elevated to NBC's morning show. Then she landed a juicy spot as host of a reality show on top of that.

"So all you have to do nowadays is sleep with the head of the division and you get the world," Ritz muttered to herself about the rumors of how Miranda Chicano actually caused the divorce of the head of the network. "I should purchase some knee pads and practice my jaw exercises. That seems to be the easiest way to get to the top."

Then Ritz let her imagination wander. Ruff *was* kind of sexy for a man in his fifties. He wisely shaved his head, which was already balding, and he worked out enough to not have a potbelly but not enough to be in really good shape. He always smelled good, too. Some people could wear Paul Sebastian and just stink. But when Ruff wore it, he owned it. He must have been wearing that scent since high school, but by now it smelled like it might be part of his own body chemistry. Ruff's hands were very strong, sexy and masculine, like Bill Clinton's. Ritz met the president at the press conference when he moved his offices to Harlem. She dusted off her press pass, which she forced herself to renew every two years just in case. Ritz made sure she got in line to shake his hand.

She instantly understood the buzz about him. He had a hypnotic air, an undeniable magnetism. And best of all, he had these big, smooth but very masculine hands—just like Ruff's.

Ritz quickly snapped herself back to reality.

"What in the hell am I thinking?!" she said to herself. "I'll find another way. I have to find a way to get to the next level."

During her shift the next night, Ritz got the first edition of the next day's papers. The early edition of the *Daily News* and *USA Today* and the *Post* were usually on her desk by nine or nine-thirty P.M. On Thursdays, she made sure the night intern brought her the *Star*, the *Enquirer*, and the *Globe*. She needed to stay abreast of the real news, the news that was popular with the people. Ritz had started delving into gossip on the air about a year before—simply to cut the boredom. It was fun reading about the outrageous lives of some of these celebrities, and it kept Ritz and her listeners in a frenzy, kicking these rich folks when they were down.

Ritz liked asking questions like "Why do you think Eddie Murphy's wife *really* left him?" Then she would invite her callers to explore all of the rumors and all of the options. Doing her show was nothing but pure fun.

On this night, with her shift heading into the final hour, Ritz picked up *USA Today*. On the front cover in full color was a photo of Delilah Summers. Her article was an "explosive ABC special report" with the new Palestinian leader. The interview was billed as "changing the face of the Middle East conflict."

When Ritz came back from her break, she was still thinking about how big Delilah Summers had become. Delilah was the hottest news interviewer in the country and had even overtaken Barbara Walters. Many saw Delilah Summers as not only the heir apparent who would move in when Barbara Walters retired but as the one who could actually push Walters into retirement. Delilah had easily bagged seven major interviews that others wanted last year, including an exclusive with the president, an interview with Saddam Hussein in prison, and the bombshell of bombshells, the interview with Whitney Houston that all but finished the diva's career. Delilah Summers was a superstar.

"Delilah Summers," Ritz cooed the name over the air after she came back from her song set. Ritz would normally give the time and temperature and maybe a little banter about something in the news, but Ritz had Delilah on the brain.

"Can you all believe that she and I went to school together? She's a little older than I am, of course," Ritz said. "Boy, was Delilah Summers a wild one! Now look at her—all famous and serious and everything! Wow, people sure do change. Or do they?"

Inside, Ritz had sharp pangs of jealousy. Delilah Summers was not only wild, she was reckless. She was the one at the frat parties getting pissy drunk. Not Ritz. Delilah went through boys the way dudes go through women. Not Ritz. And Delilah was a real bitch. She had been very condescending to Ritz from the day they met. They'd been college roommates.

While Ritz was a little bit shy and a little bit corny back then, Delilah capitalized on those traits. Ritz became her doormat and her confidante.

One night Ritz played lookout for Delilah while she gave a blowjob to the program director of their campus radio station. He also just happened to be the husband of the dean of the media department who was a chaperone at the party. Delilah did a good job of making everyone believe she was the golden girl—the consummate talent, the ultimate professional. She was good at fooling people into thinking she even had morals and scruples. Nobody got to see the real Delilah—except the people who were involved with her sexcapades. And Ritz, of course.

Ritz knew things about Delilah that she had vowed to take to her grave, but now those same secrets were scratching at the surface, itching to get out.

Delilah had the complete package. She had the look— clean, All-American. Her hair was always well done. She kept it cut just above the shoulder in a simple pageboy that framed her face. Delilah was pretty, even during the 1980s when everybody looked bad with the big hair and horrible fashions (remember Gloria Vanderbilt jeans?). Delilah had style. But she also had substance. She could read copy better than anyone, and her delivery was flawless.

Delilah also understood a few things that Ritz was only beginning to understand: It's not what you know, it's *who* you know. Or better yet, it's who knows you. Delilah Summers seemed to make it her business to be known by all the right people. While Ritz knew that deep inside herself, there was a diva waiting to get out, she hadn't quite allowed her to be free. Delilah, however, flexed her diva muscle until it bulged.

In addition to spending time partying and socializing with the "right" people, Delilah also put a lot of time into polishing her act. She perfected everything from her diction to her looks. Before they graduated, Delilah had already landed a gig at a local television station working as a news anchor. Within in a year, she had made it to a major network as a reporter, and a year later she was sitting comfortably in the anchor's seat.

She had all of the skills of Barbara Walters, without the lisp. And even though Delilah was a classic beauty, she was nonthreatening. Where Katie Couric was cute—some even thought *too* cute to be taken seriously—Delilah crossed over. Early in her career she landed an interview with the vice president of the United States. He was one of the more reclusive types who never granted interviews. He didn't want to be president and shunned the spotlight. But he agreed to an exclusive with Delilah Summers that instantly made her a player.

Over the years, the name Delilah Summers became synonymous with big interviews—from the exposé with Michael Jackson, to her gripping interview with Fidel Castro in Cuba.

Delilah Summers was at the top of her game. Ritz Harper was floundering—doing nights at an urban station with no upside. And on this particular night, Ritz decided to shift the balance as she reminisced over the airwaves about her old friend.

"I remember one night Delilah got so high that she passed out on the steps of our dorm," Ritz said. "People were walking over her like she was a lump of garbage. Can you imagine that? I remember when she was giving head to every star on the basketball team. Now she's sitting down with heads of state. Oops, did I say that?!"

She certainly did. And it felt good. Ritz felt euphoric as she purged the years of envy from her spirit, as she regurgitated the years of frustration. For years Ritz had wondered: What if? What if *she* had done the things that Delilah had done? Would she be a star today, too?

But the burning question for Ritz in that moment was: How solid was Delilah Summers's star? Could it actually fall?

"Yeah, Delilah Summers . . . she may be a spokesperson for safe sex now, but I know she turned a trick once and there was nothing safe about it. She needed money to pay for her room and her books and, well, she did what she had to do. Then a few weeks later she finds out she's pregnant, something about the rubber breaking. Well, I had to accompany her to an abortion clinic not too long after that!"

Ritz was *not* making it up. Delilah Summers had had an abortion, and Ritz had driven her home. Ritz was not just her roommate, she was Delilah's only female friend. Delilah, who didn't particular care for women, shunned female friendship. Ritz put up with a lot to be her friend. Ritz was so enamored of Delilah, so in awe of her. She wanted to be like her and at the same time wanted to be nothing like her. Ritz thought she was better than Delilah. She couldn't do what Delilah seemed to be willing to do. But Ritz was also so intimidated by Delilah that she felt compelled to take her shit and keep her secrets. Ritz couldn't even talk about her until this toasty summer night many years later when it all came spilling out.

"I'm just sick of all the hypocrites out there—all of these so-called leaders who come off all perfect. I'm sick of the Jesse Jacksons and his illegitimate baby. I'm sick of Al Sharpton and . . . well, where do I start? And I'm sick of Delilah Summers!"

The phone lines started to light up. Ritz had almost forgotten that she was on the air. She had missed her break and had talked through two song rotations. The night program pretty much ran without much interference. There wasn't a producer, and Ritz operated her own boards.

"Ritz, I am sick of these people, too!" cried Terry in the Bronx. "You go! It's nice to know there's someone out there keeping it real!"

"Thank you, Terry!" Ritz said. "And what's your favorite station?"

"WHOT! The place to be," Terry said on cue. Ritz never forgot to get the station ID in. Even though she veered from the program—which was to promote the station, make a few comments, and announce the next songs—she was still the consummate radio professional. She always got in her radio obligatories. "Next caller, you're on with Ritz!"

"Yo, Ritz, you need to stop hating!" Gary from Brooklyn said. "I can't even see Delilah Summers doing any of that! That's why black people can't get ahead now—there's always someone there to knock them down."

"No, Gary, I'm talking about someone who gave too much head," Ritz shot back. "And as far as black people holding each other down—aren't you tired of having people represent you who are frauds? Let's really keep it real tonight. Aren't you sick and tired? You should be. I know I am. It's time for us to start telling it like it is. And hopefully raise the standard around here. That's right! I'm going to tell it all tonight. What do I have, ten more minutes? Well, I have at least ten more *days* of stories about Delilah Summers. So y'all need to stay tuned. When we come back from this break, I'm going to tell you about the girlfriend she had in college—and I mean *girl*friend!"

By this time, all nine lines were blinking furiously. Ritz had to go to a commercial break to answer the phones. On a normal night she might average a few calls. The phone lines would light up when there was a contest or a give-away, but it was pretty much quiet in the studio. But on this blistering early August night, it seemed like the Fourth of July the way the lines were flaring.

The first line she answered was the only one that mattered—the hot line. That was the red blinking light from her bosses.

"Uh-oh!" she thought. "I done did it now!" Ritz wasn't

sure which boss would be on the other end, and she was very nervous. She picked up the hot line not knowing if this was the beginning or the end of her career.

"Ritz, what the fuck! What are you talking about?!" Ruff exclaimed. "But before you answer, I need to know: Is any of this shit true?!"

"Hey, Ruff," Ritz said coyly. "I didn't know you listened to the night shift."

"Stop playing! Are you trying to get us sued?"

"You know me better than that!" Ritz said. "It's all true. I wouldn't be saying it if it wasn't true."

"Girl, it better be!" he said. "You know how powerful Delilah Summers is. If she comes after us and your shit ain't right, then that's our ass! Or should I say that's *your* ass!"

"Ruff, Ruff, Ruff, you worry too much," Ritz said. "If you want, I can bring on eyewitnesses!"

"Word?" Ruff was very corporate, but when he was comfortable, his roots would show. And he was very comfortable with Ritz. "Okay, kiddo, you better drink lots of coffee because you're going on the morning show to break this story again. Then after that we need to talk."

Shocky John did the morning show on WHOT. He had just come back to New York after leaving because of a parody he'd done on the tsunami victims, which was too tasteless even for his audience. The station felt the heat of the protests, particularly from the Asian community, and they suspended him indefinitely. He quickly landed a job in Philly, where his ratings shot to number one. Ratings *are* king, and

Shocky John was welcomed back to New York City in almost no time with open arms. All was forgiven.

Shocky John and now Dr. Mark got the WHOT billboards and the commercials. They did most of the appearances and promos. They were the stars. But at seven in the morning, Ritz Harper was going to get her fifteen minutes. She spent the final ten minutes of her show feeling as if she had smoked a whole blunt, as she fielded calls and got sassier by the minute. Afterward she didn't want to go home.

"What if I oversleep?" she thought. It was midnight and Ritz usually stayed up until about three watching talk show reruns, the *Honeymooner*, and *Bewitched*. She loved Samantha's antics. Then she'd doze off with the TV still on.

But tonight Ritz couldn't sleep, so she would take Ruff's advice and get some coffee and stay up. She sat up with the overnight jock, the Sandman, who played mostly slow-ass classic R&B songs that put people to sleep. He was a real character, and Ritz loved him. Sandman had done overnights at the station for more than fifteen years. He was a staple. Ritz sat with Sandman and talked about the business, about his days when Frankie Crocker was the star of WHOT. And she daydreamed about seven A.M.

But Ritz's big day started around twelve-thirty A.M., when a call came in from the *New York Post* for her. They were running a story on the front page about the wild and sexually explicit past of Delilah Summers and they wanted a quote. A *quote?*

"Miss Harper, what else can you tell us about Delilah Summers?" night editor James Hairston asked. "We're running with this for our front page. We got a tip and listened to your program. Pretty explosive stuff!"

"Well, if you want to know more, you have to listen at seven. I'll be on the morning show exposing even more," Ritz said. "In the meantime, I'll leave you with this: It's all true!"

And she hung up. Ritz was beginning to love her flair for the dramatic. She was getting butterflies thinking about what would come next. The final-edition papers were delivered at five-fifteen in the morning. And the station got them all: *Daily News, USA Today, Newsday, The New York Times,* and *The Post.* She rifled through to grab a *Post,* and there it was: "Exclusive: Delilah Summers Goes Down!"

"The *Post* always did have a way with words," Ritz thought. "And how are they going to call it their exclusive? That shit was *my* exclusive!"

Then she turned to the story and skipped through the blah, blah, blah to get to her quote.

"Yep, they spelled my name right!" She smiled with satisfaction.

Around five-thirty, the morning team started to roll in. They didn't need much prep time. They had their show down to a science. Shocky John would say something outrageous, and his two sidekicks would laugh. Shocky was an arrogant bastard with not much time for other people in the business. But on this morning he actually acknowledged Ritz.

"What's up, star!" he said. "I hear you're in the giant-slaying business. I'm jealous, and I can't wait to talk to you more about that Summers bitch."

Every woman was a "bitch" or a "ho" to Shocky. He even referred to the First Lady and Oprah as "those bitches!" Ritz didn't really like Shocky. But his numbers made him a force to be reckoned with and an ass to be kissed. For now.

"Oh, Shocky, I can't wait to go on with you," she said. "Thanks for having me."

"Don't thank me," he said. "I didn't have a choice, not that I minded. That was all Ruff."

On Shocky's show, Ritz dropped more bombs about Delilah Summers. And in one hour she established herself as the next "it" thing in radio. Ruff was waiting for Ritz after the show, and they talked about a raise—nearly thirty thousand dollars more—and a promise of an eventual move to afternoons. But she had to prove herself. How could she top the Delilah Summers exposé?

Ritz had no idea.

4

"Ritgina Dolores Harper!" There was a long pause. Ritz was happy to hear from her aunt, but when she heard her full name, she knew she was in trouble. It was certainly not the usual loving, sweet Auntie M tone Ritz always looked forward to. Ritz's smile turned into a frown. That, coupled with not getting a minute of sleep, had Ritz on edge. She should have been riding high, having rocked the morning show. She was so excited. She didn't get home until just before nine. Ritz was looking forward to speaking with her aunt about the excitement over the last ten hours.

"I . . . we . . . are very disappointed by what we heard last night," Aunt Madalyn said.

Ritz didn't expect her aunt and uncle to approve of her demolition of Delilah Summers. But she thought they would at least understand. Radio was changing. It *had* changed. And

WENDY WILLIAMS *and* KAREN HUNTER ☆ *43*

if Ritz was going to take it to the next level, she had to make some moves. Her bomb-drop on Delilah Summers was not just a move, it was a giant step that could actually give her what she wanted, if not at WHOT, then somewhere else.

"Auntie M, I know that you're not happy with how I conducted myself last night, but you have to know that this will all turn out well for me," Ritz said.

"We did not raise you like that," said Aunt Madalyn. Ritz could tell that Uncle Cecil was somewhere in the background. While he never got involved on the rare occasions when Ritz and her aunt had a disagreement, she could feel his presence.

"How could you get on the air and talk about somebody like that? I thought you and that girl were friends. She has eaten at our dinner table, Ritz. Did she do something to you? Ritgina, I don't think I ever heard you sound so hateful. I know your mother would be crushed and embarrassed to hear you performing this way, God bless her soul."

Ritz choked back tears. It was the first time her aunt called out her mother's memory in such a way. Aunt Madalyn had always used her mother as a source of strength and motivation, and it always worked. When Aunt Madalyn said, "Your mother is watching!" it was always a source of pride for Ritz, whose heart would be filled by the notion that her mother was somewhere looking down on her little girl who was making it despite the odds. But not today.

Today Aunt Madalyn's words were breaking Ritz's heart. Ritz was embarrassed by what she had done. But that embarrassment quickly turned to anger. If she was ever going to take another breath after her aunt's blow, Ritz decided she would have to swing back hard.

"You know what? I'm sick of you talking about my mother," Ritz said. "That was *my* mother. She raised me to fight for myself. She raised me to say whatever was on mind. What do you want me to be, some poor old church lady just making ends meet for the rest of my life? With all of that 'God will provide' bullshit? That's some bullshit to go along with your slave mentality. You didn't raise me. My mother raised me, and she didn't raise a slave!"

With those words, Ritz slammed down the phone. And as her heart hardened further, she was also slamming closed a chapter in her life. It would be the second time in her life she felt so much pain.

But it would not be the last.

5

JUNE 2001

Chas James was one of the biggest party promoters in New York. He managed to remain somewhat anonymous by having a string of party-promoter wannabes around as fronts, out in the public seemingly making things happen while Chas played puppetmaster actually making things happen. Chas liked being behind the scenes. He liked being able to stand in the club near the deejay booth and watch the success of his handiwork without being the center of attention, without working the room.

During the heyday of Studio 54 and the Garage, the promoters were faces that clubgoers recognized. Chas was known by name only. It allowed him to go places without people worrying about him. He was also able to see things few got to see. Chas kept a low profile because it was good for business.

In his private life, he was flamboyant and loved attention. But he was too smart to let his own desire for the limelight get in the way of making money.

Everybody who was anybody wanted to get into Chas's parties, especially when he had one at Bungalow 8, where you needed a special key to get in. A-list celebrities were always present. Chas would hover around like a black ghost making sure things ran smoothly. His reputation was everything. He was such a perfectionist that he watched over everything at his parties, from the bar to the bathroom.

Tuesday's were Chas's party nights at Bungalow 8. He was able to get a great deal on the rate because it was not a hot party night. He was astute enough to know that in New York, though, there was never an "off" party night. If you threw the right kind of party, people would show up. The first Tuesday out, Chas netted more than fifteen thousand. He made his real money, however, promoting undercover parties for elite actors, ballplayers, and entertainers. These parties were for gentlemen only and were by invitation only. They were very, very private—so private that those invited could not bring a guest. If your name wasn't on the list, you didn't get in—no exceptions.

Chas started throwing these "undercover" parties after attending one four years earlier at a private loft in downtown Manhattan. He was placed on a list through one of his club connections, and when he arrived at the double metal doors, the bouncer/doorman, who was about six-four and three hundred pounds of muscle, handed him a brown paper bag and told him to take off everything—including his underwear—and place his things in the bag. He also was given a rich, white terry-cloth robe, like the ones at the Plaza or the Four Seasons. When he returned with his bag wearing the robe, he was given a number, which he placed in the pocket of the robe.

Inside, the loft was divided into dimly lit "stations" set up for various activities. Chas could choose from the "voyeur station," where he could watch from a chair in the corner of the room while different men participated in various sexual activities. There was the "orgy room," where Chas could jump in and join the fun—whatever fun he chose. There was the "bottoms-up room," where men could have their choice of being a "bottom" or a "top." Bottoms were required to be naked with their bottoms in the air. Tops would have their pick of which bottom they wanted to "tap." Chas switch hit from time to time, depending on his mood. He chose to sample the "one-on-one" room, designed as a mini club scene where men got to chat and know one another.

This is where he first met Ivan Richardson. The architect from Miami had never been to a place like this before. He was nervous and very out of his element. His buddy from school, Gerard, told him he was taking him someplace special. He had a guest pass and wanted to show Ivan a good time. Once he stepped into the room, Ivan had second thoughts and then a third thought: "You only live once. What the hell!"

After hurriedly checking out each station, Ivan rushed to what he considered the only safe room in the place. He went straight for a table in the corner, leaving his friend in the voyeur room. Ivan hadn't had a relationship for a year and was not into casual sex. He would get through the night, he told himself, one drink at a time. Ivan ordered a Belvedere neat and sipped it while he watched the men come and go.

Chas noticed Ivan immediately. He had the same wide-eyed look Chas imagined that he had. Chas may have *felt* like he had a wide-eyed look, but he was too smooth for that. Chas casually walked over to Ivan's table and boldly sat down.

"Can I buy you another drink?" he asked.

"Um, I'm not quite done with this one," said Ivan.

"You're not from New York, are you?" Chas chuckled.

"What gave it away?"

"What didn't?" Both men burst out laughing.

Chas and Ivan spent the night talking about everyone in the room, including Ivan's friend who brought him. Gerard was getting to know one of the men he was watching. The room was getting quite crowded.

Chas thought Ivan was going to lose it when the star point guard from an NBA team walked into the room.

"Get the fuck out here!" Ivan said. "I had no idea!"

"How could you *not* know that?" Chas said. "Hell, man, there are so many undercover brothers in the NBA, it would shock the hell out of you if I started naming names."

The phrase "down low" had not yet officially made its way into popular vernacular—it had not become a nationwide phenomenon yet. But the practice had been around since the Roman days, since the days before Caligula.

These seemingly straight men who seemingly enjoyed women but who also liked the company of men were not new to Chas. Most of the men he hooked up with fit this category, and he liked it that way. It was yet another way for him to be invisible. His male companions had too much to lose to be known as gay, as did just about every man in the room with Chas and Ivan that night. There were star ballers, investment bankers, entrepreneurs, and even one famous but fading soul singer—all living out their wildest fantasies or just satisfying a physical need. But all doing so undercover on the down low.

"This evening turned out to be quite interesting after all," Ivan said, after having downed his third Belvedere.

"How long are you going to be in town?" Chas asked.

"Oh, only a couple more days. I have to get back to work. Things are starting to heat up for me there."

"Well, maybe we can get together before you leave," Chas said. "I'll show you another side to New York. It'll be fun."

They exchanged numbers and Ivan got up to get his things. He was ready to go. Chas stayed around to take some mental notes. He was getting a blueprint for his own club. He made sure to pay attention to what was working—like the intimate bar area where people could get to know one another. And the things that didn't work so well—like the bottoms-up room. "That's just too much," he thought. "They can take that shit to a hotel room. Who can really get loose in an environment like that?"

A year later, Chas created the Spy Zone. His list would be so exclusive that there wouldn't be a list. Members only. The way to become a member was a secret. Chas's club was harder to get into than joining the Masons—the white Masons. It was harder to get into the Spy Zone than for Mo'Nique to squeeze her fat ass into a pair of size-four panties. The membership fee started at ten thousand dollars a month, and Chas planned to increase it each year.

Chas put a lot of money back into the club, with its secret entrances, tunnels, and exits. He made sure everything, from the open bar with the most expensive selections to the linens, was top of the line. The Spy Zone was open only once a week. The other days, Chas spent at various straight clubs around the city. Those nights were more for his amusement.

On one such night, Chas met Ritz Harper. She was still doing nights. She wasn't yet the dynamo she eventually turned into. But for Chas, there was something special about this woman. He was hanging out at his favorite spot—next to the deejay's booth—as this harried vision came in like a bat out of hell. Ritz always came late.

"Ritz Harper," Chas muttered to himself, and smiled. Few people knew what Ritz looked like, but Chas was really into the whole entertainment game. He loved the players and loved watching the plays. Ritz wasn't a real player yet, but Chas saw the potential.

Ritz was doing a promotional appearance for the station.

She was to come on the stage, give a few shout-outs to the audience, introduce the deejay, and kick it back to the studio. It was Mix-Jam Fridays broadcasting live on WHOT, where they featured three hours of club music. Ritz was late—as usual. But she made up for it with energy.

"Hey, everybody!!!!!" she shouted, pulling everything together so quickly that Chas was shocked how she went from disheveled to perfect in a split section. "You all look great. Let me hear some noise! Is Brooklyn in the house?!"

The crowd went wild.

"Let me hear from my people in Jerrrrrrsaaaay!!!!!!"

A roar went up.

"Is there anyone here from the Boogie Down?!!!!!!"

Whoops and hollers followed.

"That's more like it!" Ritz said, feeling her rhythm. "So what are we here for?" And the crowd shouted unintelligible blather.

Ritz had officially gotten the party started. She capped it off with a few more borough calls and some birthday shout-outs, which always were a hit, and she was ready to send it back to the studio for the music.

"That's right! We're here to PAR-TAY! So let's get this party started, right?" Ritz said as the deejay started his set. "Let's hear it for Deejay Smooooooooooooth!" And the crowd went wild again.

Ritz walked behind the deejay booth and took a deep breath. She didn't even notice Chas in the corner looking at her.

"Nice job, Miss Thing," Chas said.

"Why, thank you," Ritz said, smiling.

"I'm Chas. And I like your style. You have a real future."

"*This* I know," Ritz shot back, halfway insulted but trying not to look it.

"This is a tough business," Chas said, shouting over the music. "I think I can help you."

"And what do you do? What are you, a manager or something?"

"No, I'm even better than that. Let's talk tomorrow before your show and I'll tell you what I'm thinking. This is not a good place to conduct business."

Business? "Who the hell did he think he was, P. Diddy or something?" Ritz thought. But she liked his boldness. Chas was one of the most confident and sure people Ritz had ever met. "If just a little of that could rub off on me," Ritz thought. It was worth hearing him out. She took his number and they agreed to meet at the Starbucks on the ground floor of the radio station on Thirty-fourth Street.

Those first cups of coffee turned into a friendship, or at least a budding partnership. Chas gave Ritz insight into herself that no one else had. He told her that she had to do something about her look.

"Honey, I know it's radio, but you have to *think* bigger than that if you want to *be* bigger than that," Chas told her.

He had Ritz thinking about making some serious changes. At five foot eight, Ritz was above average in height, but everything else about her was average. Her hair was boring.

Her body was nothing special. She carried herself like a frump. Chas put her in contact with a style guru of his, Darryl Brown, who connected her with a hairstylist who gave Ritz a whole new look. It was over-the-top—long, honey-blond, and big—and it suited Ritz to a T.

After the hair, Ritz started thinking about increasing her frontal net worth—a double D increase, to be exact. She got her boob job on a payment plan.

"Think of it as an investment," Chas said. "Trust me, it will pay off!"

Ritz's transformation, except for the boob job, which took everyone by surprise, was subtle and gradual. It started the night she and Chas met, and it solidified when Ritz made up her mind that her career would take off—if it killed her.

Her mother used to tell her about the five P's that would carry her through life: Proper Planning Prevents Poor Performance.

"Ritzy, if you plan properly and are prepared, you can handle anything. Most people fail because they fail to plan."

It was a cliché Ritz never forgot. When she decided she wanted to be in radio, she didn't just jump in front of a microphone and start talking. She had internships and learned the game from the inside out.

Over a six-month period, she started looking better and better. By the time she pushed through with the explosive Delilah Summers exposé, Ritz was "runway ready." It was something Chas preached that complimented her mother's sentiments.

"Girl, you must always, always be runway ready," Chas would say. "You never ever know when you'll be called on to be on television or do an interview or just get caught out in the street. You want to always be runway ready."

Now Ritz was more than runway ready; she was ready-ready, thanks to Chas. He liked his role as Pygmalion. He loved his deep-chocolate Eliza Doolittle. Perhaps working with Chas over those months gave Ritz the confidence to break out of her shell and do something radical. The physical changes she made had spilled over into her personality.

Ritz's move from the night shift was swift. Ruff promised the move would be "soon," but she never anticipated it would take literally three days after her bomb-drop on Delilah Summers for her to be given the coveted afternoon drive shift. Radio was cruel in that way. Dr. Mark, who had decent ratings and quite a following, was summarily moved to Ritz's shift. He still had a year left on his contract that the station did not want to eat. In radio, the drive for the best ratings was nasty. WHOT saw Ritz as their next cash cow.

"This must have been the way that little William Hung felt on *American Idol* or that Omarosa from the *Apprentice*," she thought with amusement. "Fuck that! I actually have talent! I deserve this."

Ritz started doing newspaper interviews and magazine interviews. She was featured on *Extra* and *Access Hollywood*.

VH1 was hollering for her. She even made an appearance on Bill O'Reilly's show to talk about the shameful state of the news field. There was Stephen Glass, Mike Barnicle, Jayson Blair, Dan Rather, and now Delilah Summers.

Ritz's relationship with Ruff changed instantly. Soon he'd turn into Ritz's very own public relations rep as he and Ritz had daily discussions about which shows to do and which ones to avoid and what angle to take.

"Tell the *Enquirer* to fuck off," Ruff said. "We have to have *some* limits! But O'Reilly?! Damn, girl. You have arrived!"

"Shiiiit," Ritz said. "He ought to add his own ass to that list of fallen news heroes. Didn't he have to settle out of court with some chick who accused him of sexual harassment? That's the kind of shit I'm talking about!"

"Easy, killa," Ruff said. "You're going to go on *The O'Reilly Factor* and you're going to make nice. He has five million viewers, and we want to get a few of them on WHOT. You can work that. I know you can."

"Why, of course," Ritz purred. "You know I will make it do what it do."

And they both broke out into a private chuckle. Soon Ruff realized that he really liked Ritz. She was "a bitch with balls," a woman after his own heart—tough enough not to let people take advantage of her, but soft enough to know how to be a lady. Ritz liked Ruff, too. He was the first and only boss she had who was completely up front and honest with her.

Ritz found most people in radio to be very shady. "Hell, it's that way with most people in life," she thought. They would smile in your face, telling you everything was fine, while taking out a knife to stab you in the back. Not Ruff. He would look you square in the face and stab you in the front—if that's what he was going to do. Ritz always knew where she stood with him, and he never lied to her.

Their relationship didn't progress beyond mutual admiration. Ritz had a rule about crossing lines with her bosses. Ruff was from the rules-were-made-to-be-broken school. He would break all of the rules for Ritz, but she would have to make the first move—which she was not inclined to do. Until she did come around, Ruff was relegated to chief cheerleader and mentor and, of course, boss.

It was one in the afternoon, an hour before Ritz's debut in her new slot. Ruff made sure she had everything she needed and everything she wanted—including Chas. She had convinced Ruff that she needed a producer to take her to the top. Chas didn't have the typical radio experience, but Ruff hired him anyway.

"I trust you, Ritz," he said. "But if it doesn't work, I'm bouncing both of your asses out of here! Don't fuck this up."

She sat on the toilet of the handicapped stall in the station's bathroom. She was nauseous and didn't want anyone to see her looking anything but confident. Her hands were sweating and for perhaps the first time in her adult life Ritz was scared.

"What if?" was the question that kept swirling around her head. "What if I *do* fuck this up?"

She felt completely alone. Ritz didn't have Tracee to lean

on. She wasn't speaking to her Aunt Madalyn. She couldn't dare tell Ruff about her fears. She could talk to Chas, but he would tell her what she already knew: "Girl, you better suck this up. You only have one chance to make a good first impression, and this is your chance!"

Ritz gluped down some Maalox that she had in her bag just in case, splashed her face with cold water, reapplied her makeup, and got ready for the debut of the *Ritz Harper Excursion: One Trip You Will Never Forget!* She and Chas came up with that one in a brainstorming session over the weekend. He coached her on how she would present her show with drama and pomp. He even lined up some explosive guests for her debut week. Everything was planned to the letter. But there was still that little voice inside of Ritz, that little voice of doubt.

Ritz's first hour on the air went smoothly. She started off chatting with her new listeners and talking about how excited she was to be there with them. She invited them to call in. Ritz loved talking to "her people," as she referred to the loyal listeners of her night crew. She was determined to create the same family-style environment in the afternoons, as well.

"You're on with Ritz, who's this?"

"Bitch, who the fuck do you think you are!" It was Delilah Summers. Ritz was thankful for the seven-second delay and even more thankful for Aaron, the engineer who was a holdover from Dr. Mark's show. He was a pro and not only quick on the bleep button, but also smart. He left in the FCC-acceptable "bitch" and only bleeped out the "fuck," so the audience could get the full dramatic effect.

"Delilah?" Ritz said in the sweetest voice she could muster. "Girl, long time no speak! How are you! What can I do for you?"

"Oh, you've done enough, bitch!" Delilah's speech was slurring, and it was clear that she was under the influence of alcohol. "I ought to come down to that station and fuck you up. Better yet, I wouldn't dirty my hands on your shanky ass! Bitch!"

It was quite a departure from the usually well-spoken perfect diction that defined Delilah Summers. She sounded like the straight-up from Bed-Stuy, Brooklyn, chick that she really was. Like Tina Turner, Eartha Kitt, Maya Angelou, and even Madonna, Delilah Summers had found a way to erase all ethnicity from her vernacular and delivery. She was the quintessential crossover personality. But one call to Ritz erased all remnants of the image she had worked so many years to craft. Ritz put her business in the street and her career in the toilet, and with one call, Delilah Summers flushed it.

"You are such a jealous, grimy bitch," Delilah continued. "After all I've done for you . . . Ritz, you will get yours. You *will* get yours!"

And she hung up.

"Well!" Ritz said. "I guess she was mad, huh? I don't blame her. But I will tell you all this: What hasn't caught you hasn't passed you. She shouldn't be mad at me, she should be mad at her damn self."

Deep down inside (and that place was growing deeper by the day), Ritz did feel a little remorse. She and Delilah had been friends—even if it wasn't an equal relationship. Delilah had worked hard, and Ritz had learned a lot from her. But oh well. If bringing Delilah down put Ritz on top, so be it.

"I deserve being here more," Ritz said to herself, trying to convince herself of that. "She didn't look out for me. Not once. Fuck her!"

The phone lines lit up just as they had the first night of the Delilah Summers scandal. And there were calls from all of the entertainment and newsmagazine shows—including *60 Minutes*—wanting a response from Ritz. It was announced that afternoon that Delilah Summers was let out of her network contract for "personal" reasons. While her star had fallen, Ritz's was on the rise.

ON THE AIR

"You're on with Ritz. What's on your mind?"

"Hey, girl! This is Sheila from Atlanta, and I have a problem. I have been seeing this man for about a year now. But I met this other guy and I can't stop thinking about *him*."

"Okay?" Ritz said. "This man you've been seeing, would you consider him your boyfriend? I mean, you say you're *seeing* him, but are you in love with him? Are you all talking marriage? What's the deal?"

"We have a little boy together and yes, we're talking marriage."

"Oh my!" Ritz purred.

"I love him," Sheila from Atlanta said. "I really do. He's a great father. He's a great boyfriend. But we're not compatible in bed. I want it all of the time and he doesn't."

"Ooooooh!" Aaron, the engineer, howled. Ritz kept his mike open because Aaron was good for a dumb-ass comment or sound effect during the show. He also provided lots of color that Ritz liked.

"Yes, you *do* have a problem," Ritz said.

"I don't want to cheat on him, but this other man who I met online is so freaking sexy. We've talked on the phone, and Ritz, without even touching me, he made me come harder than I ever came with my man."

Aaron was quick on the "beep" button when she said "come." He was always ready. Ever since that whole Janet Jackson titty flack at Super Bowl XXXVIII and Howard Stern's many, many violations that cost him and his station millions, Ritz didn't take any chances. She skirted the line often but she never crossed it. She wasn't messing with the FCC, which she called the Fucking Cunt Commission.

"Fantasies are fine," Ritz said. "In fact, I think they're healthy. And as long as you two don't actually get together, I say use your Internet jump-off and fantasize about him while you're in bed with your man. See if that works. And during those times when your man isn't in the mood, I suggest you get you a Jackrabbit vibrator. They have a new one out called the Impulse and, girl! Well! I won't tell you . . . you go see for yourself. And if I were you, I would pull out my old Jackrabbit and go to work in front of him. Trust me, if he doesn't get the hint, then he's not a real man. And if it doesn't work—I mean, everything I've told you—holla back."

"Thank you, Ritz!"

"Oh, my pleasure," Ritz said. "I mean, it will be *your* pleasure!"

"Ooooh!" Aaron howled again.

"Next caller," Ritz said. "You're on with Ritz!"

☆   ★   ☆

During the first break, Ritz took a sip of her diet Pepsi, one of five she drank during her shift.

"Jamie, I'm ready for another," Ritz yelled to her latest intern, who was busy getting the hundreds of faxes coming in, checking the e-mails, answering the phones, and loving it.

"Okay, Ritz," Jamie said, never letting anyone see her sweat. Jamie was a third-year student at New York University and ambitious as hell. Her banker father taught her the No. 1 rule of success: Identify the power and stay close to it. "It's the only way you will conquer it, sweetie. You have to be at the right hand of power."

Jamie went above and beyond the call of duty for Ritz and never complained. In fact, she always seemed to have a smile even when Ritz humiliated her on the air.

"Um, intern!" Ritz would scream on the air. "This diet Pepsi is not cold enough! What's your problem?! People, can I tell you how hard it is to find good help?"

Jamie never showed any frustration. She would just go back and get a colder diet Pepsi, pressing it against her arm to make sure that it was indeed cold. She then put the cool one in the tiny freezer in the half fridge in the Ritz's "office." The station pimped out an entire large corner of the utility room to give Ritz her own space. All of the corner offices were taken by executives. Ritz's makeshift office turned out to be among the biggest. It was definitely the most colorful. She decorated it with an animal-print rug, painted the walls pink—her favorite color—and adorned them with photos from her most famous interviews. She had pictures with Angela Bassett and Janet Jackson, O.J. Simpson (one of her favorites. She was surprised by how sexy he was), and even Jennifer Lopez, whom Ritz interviewed when J. Lo was the hottest thing going—back when she was with P. Diddy, who was just Puffy then and Ritz was still doing nights. Now the tables had turned but J. Lo was still one of her favorites.

Jamie rushed back to the studio with the ice-cold diet Pepsi and discreetly placed it on the desk in front of Ritz, who picked it up without even looking.

"Now that's better, intern," said Ritz, who never called her interns by name on the air because they never lasted longer than three months and she didn't want her audience to get attached. Keeping them nameless kept them anonymous and, therefore, nobodies. But Jamie was in her sixth month. Ritz, despite the hard time she gave her, actually adored her.

"That Jamie is trying to make herself invaluable," Ritz told Chas after the girl's first week on the job.

"This one may be a keeper," Chas said.

"Nah, I doubt that," Ritz said, not wanting to concede.

But when Jamie's three-month stint was up, no one said any-thing. They just kept her on.

After slipping the icy diet Pepsi into place at Ritz's right hand, out of the way of the stack of faxes, magazines, and other papers, Jamie took her seat to finish screening calls. The phone lines never stopped, and it was Jamie's job to weed out the nut jobs from the whack jobs. The whack jobs were the most coveted callers—like James in St. Louis who once called to get advice about what to do about his fifteen-inch penis. He was having a hard time, *literally*, getting a steady girlfriend. And there was Stephanie from Westchester, who had slept with practically every star athlete in the world. She was always good for some gossip about someone no one ever expected to hear about.

The nut jobs were plentiful. These were the people who just wanted to be on the air and really had nothing to say. They were just plain crazy. That kind of crazy didn't make for good radio. It was tedious.

But Ritz loved the whack jobs. She even got a collect call once from a maximum security prison. Jamie wasn't sure whether to let it through, but her instincts never let her down.

"Ritz, we have a confessed pedophile on line three, calling collect," Jamie said, hoping not to get yelled at. "Maybe you should take him next!"

"Excellent!" Ritz said.

"Hey, this is Ritz, who's this?"

"This is Gene. I'm calling from Dannemora," he said.

"That's a prison!"

"Yeah. I hear you talking about Michael Jackson and what you would like to do with pedophiles, and I'm here to tell you, none of that shit you're talking will work."

Aaron was ready on the bleep button.

"When I raped my daughter, I knew inside it was wrong but I couldn't help myself. I can't explain it. It's like another thing came over me and I was watching myself doing it, telling myself not to, but I wouldn't listen."

"You raped your daughter?" Ritz asked, trying not to let too much disgust show in her voice. She hated this man whom she had never met, but she wanted him to stay on the line. She didn't want to lose him—not until she milked him for his story.

"Yeah, and I kept doing it," he said.

"Did she tell on you?"

"Nah, not at all. She thought it was her fault. I was good at convincing her of that."

"So how did you end up in jail?"

"I raped my girlfriend after the bitch pissed me off. She went to the cops, the bitch!"

"How long are you in for?" Ritz asked.

"Oh, since this is the second time I got caught, I got twenty-five years. They have me in some treatment, group-therapy thing where I have to talk about my issues with other rapists and pedophiles."

"So how do the other inmates treat you?"

"Oh, I'm not fucking with them and they don't fuck with

me," he said. "I know they say that people like me get raped in prison—but it ain't happened yet. And I don't see it happening."

"That's a shame," Ritz slipped out. "So you say my solution—castration—won't work?"

"Nah."

"But wouldn't that be getting rid of the weapon?"

"Nah, Ritz. The weapon ain't between my legs. The weapon is between my ears. You have to change the way a man thinks. Even if he don't have a dick, he will find another way to rape if his mind ain't right."

"Is your mind right?"

"Not yet. I belong in jail. I ain't ready to get out. I would rape again, I believe."

"Wow, that's real honest of you."

"Well, you say you like to keep it real. That's as real as it gets."

"It sure is! You're listening to the *Ritz Harper Excursion,* better than any trip you'll take, y'all. And we'll be back after these messages!"

The red "On Air" sign went out as Aaron played bumper music leading into the commercial set.

"What the fuck?!" Ritz said. "I'm still shaking."

"Yo, dude was mad icy," Aaron chimed in.

"I'm entering that segment for the Air Awards," Chas said, always thinking about the show and the product. "That was some gripping shit."

"Where's the Moët?" Ritz said. "After that, I need something a little stronger than soda. Besides, isn't my girl coming any minute?"

The studio was abuzz over the arrival of Mariah Carey— who might be the only guest who could top the pedophile. She was one of Ritz's favorite people to interview because she was one of the few "in the business" Ritz actually liked and respected.

Advice was just one of the features that had catapulted the *Ritz Harper Excursion* to the number-one spot. In less than a month, Ritz was syndicated to four cities—Philadelphia, Hartford, Washington, DC, and the flagship in New York. There was talk of adding ten more within the year. Other cities wanted their Ritz fix, too, but Ruff didn't want to move too fast.

People loved the advice, but the real reason they tuned in was for the celebrity interviews. Ritz had found a formula that was part Oprah Winfrey, part Jerry Springer. She got all of the high-profile artists, entertainers, and authors on her show, but there was always, always a twist—which her audience counted on. Ritz had millions of listeners, and they were all part of a special insiders' club.

Ritz had developed a secret language with her audience. When a guest was on and Ritz wanted to say something about the person without the guest knowing, she had sound effects to let the audience know what she wanted them to know.

She interviewed legendary rapper Biz Markie. He was an idol in many circles and was there to promote his new reality show. Every time Biz opened his mouth, Ritz gave him the business—one look at Aaron, and the sound of a dentist's drill would go off under whatever Biz was saying. Not once did Ritz mention that Biz Markie's mouth looked like he had been chewing metal bubblegum. She never had to say that he looked like he had gingivitis and periodontal disease. The dentist's drill said it all.

If someone was pretending to have a lot of money and was, in reality, broke, Ritz would have Aaron play the sound effect of a cash register being hurled out of a window. Cairo, from the R&B group Cotton Club, who made a solo splash in the 1990s with the biggest one-hit wonders of the decade, rolled through, and Ritz let him have it.

"I saw you on *MTV Cribs*," Ritz started. "What a gorgeous home!"

"Yeah, Cairo said. "I don't get to spend much time in it."

"True that." Ritz took off the gloves. "Word has it that day was the only time you spent in it, because that ain't your house! Now tell the truth. Your label rented it for the day. You're still living with your mama, aren't you?"

(Sound effect of the cash registering being tossed out of the window: *Cha-ching, Crash!*)

Cairo sat there speechless, glaring at Ritz. He wasn't prepared for that uppercut to his diminutive chin.

"Silence says it all," Ritz said. "Let's go to a break."

As they went to a break, Aaron played Cairo's hit song. Cairo stormed out of the studio, not saying a word. When Ritz came back, she explained his absence but also the method to her madness.

"I know some of y'all think I'm cruel," she started. "But what's cruel is lying. There are so many young people out there who think that all they need to do is become a rapper or a singer or something and they're set for life. The truth is, very few of these people really have money. The rest are projecting this image and don't have the money to keep up their lifestyle. You remember TOTAL—hit records galore, but still living in the projects. Now that's cruel. People need to keep it real!

"I mean, look at Fantasia. How in the world is she going to come out with a book—one that we are to believe she wrote without any help because hers is the only name anywhere on it—and she can't read."

Aaron couldn't help but chime in on this one. "Think of all of the things she missed out on—like seeing *Crouching Tiger, Hidden Dragon*. That was a good movie, she never got to see because it has subtitles."

"That's a good one!" Ritz said, laughing heartily. "I wonder if she ever wrote a love letter. Or imagine how many boyfriends broke up with the poor girl in a letter and she never even knew it."

"She ain't never played Scrabble. The girl ain't never played Scrabble!"

"Aaron, stop it!" Ritz howled. "I can't take it."

"And let's not talk about *Jeopardy* or *Wheel of Fortune*. Ritz, imagine her trying to buy a vowel."

"And what was her mother thinking? Fantasia Barrino? How hard is that name to spell? That child must have been having fits growing up with that one."

"Okay, Aaron, now you have crossed the line," Ritz broke in, trying to hold back the uncontrollable giggles that were building up inside. "You can't talk about her mother. That's going too far."

Aaron was on a roll. Ritz knew if she didn't stop him, he would go on for the next three hours of the show and it was only going to get worse.

Sometimes Ritz felt like she was performing a public service—keeping these celebrities in check and keeping her audience hip to what was real and what was fake. She ripped masks off for all to see the truth. She worked *for* the people.

If a male star came through who seemed a little light in the pants or to have some sugar in his tank or whom Ritz had some gossip about him being on the down low but couldn't substantiate it, she would have Aaron play the sound effect of an over-the-top gay man howling "Oooooh, how you doin'?!" The guest never had a clue. The audience did, though. And they loved it.

If Ritz had hard evidence that the male star was indeed on the down low—pretending to be straight but actually enjoying the sexual company of men—she would simply ask him. And the audience could count on Ritz for that, too.

She did have a few altercations after a celebrity got back to his or her camp and found out what really went down during the interview. One tough female rapper whom Ritz hit with the gay-man-howling sound effect—which could be used on a man or a woman—every time she opened her mouth wasn't too pleased when she found out. In fact, she came back and waited for Ritz outside of the studio, threatening to "beat the bitch's ass." The cops were called. And the next day, Big Tony was hired to sit outside of the studio during Ritz's shift. A panic button was also placed under the desk in the studio just in case things got nasty. Aaron and Chas were men, but neither had enough of a street game to handle potentially violent guests. Big Tony did.

For the most part, though, celebrities took the whole Ritz experience in stride. Most understood the rule: The only bad publicity was *no* publicity. With Ritz's five million (and growing) loyal listeners, they couldn't afford *not* to show up. Ritz had such a great relationship with her audience that if she said that a CD was hot, it shot to number one. If she said that a movie was good, it would debut at the top spot. And as for books, she was having an Oprah-like touch there, too. While some people hated Ritz, they couldn't argue with the results or the fact that her audience loved her.

The love affair began the night Ritz ruined the career of the hottest newswoman in the business. It solidified Ritz's place in the annals of radio history, but it also galvanized a relationship between her and "her people." Ritz was their hero, their champion. She was the one asking the questions they were asking in their heads. She was the one not taking any crap from these celebrities. She was weeding out the fakers from the shakers. She was the ultimate BS detector. She created an "us" against "them" club, recognizing that there were way more *uses* in the world than *thems*—the celebrities. She also recognized that while everyone wanted to be a "them," when it was clear that they couldn't, they would rather hate "them." It was fun.

The more Ritz outed or exposed celebrities, the larger her audience grew. Ritz discovered this phenomenon by accident one night, but the formula was perfected by Chas, the former party promoter privy to scandals that could take down giants.

"Girl, you better put that champagne down and get ready for Mariah," Chas said. "She just got out of her limo and is on her way up as we speak."

"Relax, baby boy," Ritz cooed. "You know mama is *always* ready."

The final commercial played and the red "On Air" sign lit up. Ritz was ready on cue.

"Welcome back to the *Excursion*, everyone. Buckle up for safety!"

Mariah burst in the door, bodyguards and entourage in tow, carrying a couple of bags from Bergdorf's and a few blue bags from Tiffany's.

"Oooooh! It's Mimi, everyone! Welcome Mariah Carey to the show!" said Ritz, as Aaron played applause under the introduction and the intro of her latest hit single. "And as usual, the diva is bearing gifts. How much do I love you?!"

The two exchanged air kisses on both cheeks as Mariah took her seat in front of the mike.

"I heard you had Moët, and you can't drink it out of just any old thing. So I stopped by Tiffany's to get us a couple of glasses," Mariah said.

"Now that's what I'm talking about . . ."

WINTER GARDEN, FLORIDA

Tracee Remington reclined in her wicker chair on the balcony of her mini-mansion overlooking the ninth hole at Stoneybrook West—a community built on a golf course. She didn't play golf but she wanted a house with a view. The lush, rolling greens and the rich golfers in their crisp golf outfits were a pleasant sight for Tracee as she sipped her green tea.

She would have to pack soon, throw a few things in a bag, and get ready—physically and mentally—to go back to New York, or the "cesspool," as she had begun to call it.

It had been a year since Tracee had been back in the Big Apple, where she'd left so much of herself. It had been a year since she walked away from success and accolades to settle into a life suited for octogenarians.

This part of Florida was coming up, but it was still very

slow. It wasn't South Beach, Miami. It wasn't quite Disney, which was only a few miles away. This was the slow South. People moved slowly, they talked slowly, they thought slowly. And Tracee loved it. It was the perfect departure from the life she left behind.

Every now and then, though, Tracee longed for New York, like the time she went to pick up a laptop from Circuit City near the Millenia Mall just outside of Orlando. The salesman, Robby, dragged himself over to help her. He bragged about being in the platinum club, meaning he was a top salesman. But when Tracee asked to feel the weight of the laptop, he had to get a manager for the keys.

"He's a good salesman, but I guess they don't trust him with the keys," Tracee thought.

She grabbed a seat when she realized that his "I'll be right back" actually meant fifteen minutes. When he came back, he had the keys to unlock the display laptop but had to go back and get the keys to get an actual new laptop from the case below. Then Robby proceeded to tell Tracee about all of the features and the free package of software. It came with everything except Microsoft Word, Excel, and PowerPoint— all of the programs she needed. Robby told her that he had a master copy that he would burn for her, and he would have it if she came back the next night and met him after he got off.

"And maybe I can take your sweet self out to dinner at Red Lobster," he said, flashing a smile with gold outlining his two front teeth.

That was it. Tracee left without the laptop and had wasted

forty-five minutes of her time. She should have known that Robby was trouble when she saw the gold fronts and the huge faux gold high school class ring with the blue stone.

"What grown man wears a high school ring?" thought Tracee.

But if that was the worst she had to deal with (and it was), she would take it. It was still better than the cesspool she left.

It had been a year in the sticks—a year away from the stress and hustle of New York City. It was a year of discovery and peace for Tracee. She focused on building her spiritual muscles. Was she strong enough to go back? She was going back, anyway. She was going to be there for her friend's big debut. But Tracee was going back for more than Ritz's Grammy red carpet event, she was going back to New York to reel her friend back in. In their last conversation, she could hear Ritz coming undone.

"I don't know what I am doing all of this for sometimes, Tray," Ritz said. "My ratings are going up. I am getting offers from everywhere. I am making more money than I ever imagined making in my entire life. But I am not happy. Why'd you have to leave?"

"Because *I* wasn't happy," Tracee said.

"*We* were happy. We were having fun. I know if you came back, things would be better."

"I couldn't hear with everything going on, Ritzy. I was drowning there."

"I don't know. Maybe when I get some time, I will come to

country-ass Winter Garden and get some fresh air and clear my head for a week."

"You need more than a week, Ritzy. In the first week it actually gets worse before it gets better."

"Then I'm staying put. I can't wait for you to get here. I think being here without the pressures of your job will be a big difference."

Tracee didn't comment. She knew that while she planned on having a good time in New York—where she still had an apartment—she was never moving back.

She admittedly had run away from there. But she knew she wouldn't be completely free until she was able to go back. After being in Florida for a year, Tracee realized that the drama wasn't connected to a place. Drama could be found anywhere, even in Winter Garden, Florida. If you looked hard enough, you could find drama at the Vatican with the pope. Tracee had stopped looking for drama. That's why she took the buyout package and paid cash for the four-bedroom, three-bath, three-car-garage house on the golf course with a balcony and a swimming pool and a bonus room. It was too much house for Tracee, but she thought she would meet someone and have enough children to fill the bedrooms. She envisioned having someone to share this exquisite home with.

Until then, it provided her with a haven—a place to detox and get the filth out of her system. Tracee even found solace in writing. She purged by keeping a journal. She thought about writing a book about her experiences—a guide for those wanting to break into the music business with inside secrets, exposing all of the evils. She knew it was sure to be a bestseller. But, for now, she was content enjoying her "retirement."

Tracee smiled as she remembered telling her mother she was retiring.

"Retiring?! Retiring?! Chile, you done lost your mind!" her mother said. "You ain't but thirty-five years old. *I* haven't even retired yet. Who the hell do you think you are?!!"

Tracee was one of the youngest executives ever at Uni-Global Music Group, which had gobbled up just about every major recording label, leaving just a few independents to fight over the scraps. She was also the one of the youngest ever to take a golden parachute—or, rather, a *platinum* parachute—when the company decided to downsize the black music department. Tracee volunteered to leave.

Tracee had met Ritz during her ascent at Uni-Global. She presided over one hit act after another, responsible for everything from refining their performance to shaping their relationships with the media. Ritz wasn't *the* Ritz Harper then. She was on the rise, but she was very much a part of the media, part of the world that Tracee's artists had to conquer.

Tracee brought up-and-comer Majita to the studio to talk about her debut album. It was routine. But during the break, Ritz pulled Tracee's collar.

"You have to tell that young lady that she needs to make

sure she has breath mints before talking to the media," Ritz said. "Can you say 'Enter the Dragon'?"

Tracee was a bit surprised; she hadn't gotten close enough to Majita to notice. She was also grateful for the honesty and even more grateful that Ritz didn't say anything about it on the air. The new Ritz would have. Tracee missed the old Ritz. She had a lot more in common with the old Ritz, who was thoughtful and honest and compassionate. She was ambitious and strong. They were two women tackling a male-dominated world. As their friendship grew, it seemed that the two of them were fighting together.

Ritz loved Tracee's realness and spirit, and Tracee could see the real Ritz through her tough exterior. They kept in contact because Tracee always seemed to have a hot artist that Ritz wanted to get on her show. Tracee made it so easy for Ritz, who was beginning to feel like she had connections.

When Tracee was promoted to head of the black music division, there was no one prouder than Ritz. This was truly the first time Ritz had a female friend she could actually let her hair down with, who was equally happy for all of the success she was experiencing. Tracee was searching spiritually and developing a better relationship with God. Some of this was rubbing off onto Ritz. Not a lot, but some.

While Ritz was not heading in the same direction as Tracee, she was a great sounding board and always had an honest response. In the months leading up to making the final decision to leave her job and New York, Tracee was wavering, searching for answers. She had dinner with Ritz at Mr. Chow's, a popular spot on tony Fifty-seventh Street, which featured pigeon on the menu.

"I can't take it anymore," Tracee said to Ritz right after she sat down.

"I can't believe you," Ritz said. "People would kill for your position. Hell, I think people *have* killed to be in your place. Why are you complaining?"

"Ritz, I can't explain it, but I feel like I'm dying—like my spirit is being squashed," Tracee said. "I'm not happy. But it's deeper than that. If I'm not covering for some rapper who has gotten himself in trouble, I'm playing interference for some singer who is cheating on his wife. And that's the mild stuff. Every day it seems like I'm laying yet another brick paving my road leading straight to hell."

"Whoa! Why you do you have to bring so much drama to everything? Girl, lighten up. It ain't that serious. Just think, if you were not in that position—making all of that money, I might add—some white boy would be sitting in that seat making all of that money. At least you care about the trifling Negroes you are forced to work with. At least you try to help them. Who else is going to do that?"

"Yeah, Ritz, I do care. I care too much. I also have to start caring about me. I don't know who I am sometimes. I am doing things I know I shouldn't, and I feel like shit about it."

"Have another drink and get some sleep and you'll feel better," Ritz said, waving for their waitress. "Can we get two more Sapphire martinis, with an extra olive. Thanks."

Tracee got some sleep that night, but she didn't feel better the next day. The next morning she decided to check out a church she had heard about—Faith Baptist. They had a new young minister. Maybe he would have some answers.

She was desperate.

9

Faith Baptist Church in Harlem was the fastest-growing church uptown. Its size rivaled the Harlem powerhouses, Riverside Church and Abyssinian Baptist Church. Pastor Edwin Lakes Sr. had started Faith Baptist more than thirty years ago with just a hundred parishioners and a dream. His sudden death left the completion of that dream on the shoulders of his son, Edwin Jr.

Edwin was anything but ready when he took over nearly seven years ago. But he had to get ready. He didn't have a choice. It was understood that he was the heir apparent and that was that. Edwin Jr. attended seminary at Drew University in Madison, New Jersey—following in the footsteps of his father, Edwin Sr., the great Reverend Dr. Samuel Proctor, and so many other prominent and powerful preachers throughout the country. He went through the motions of everything he was supposed to do, everything that was expected of him.

He went to seminary because, as the only son of Edwin Lakes, that was his legacy. But when he graduated, Edwin wasn't sure if he wanted to go into the ministry. He wasn't sure if he had the right stuff to lead a church. Hell, he wasn't sure about a lot of things.

He told his parents that he needed some time to "find himself" and decided to move to Miami, Florida, where he could enjoy the weather and be free from his father's awesome shadow and the pressure of being his son. He had never been to Miami but from all he'd read and seen on television, it was a place where he could have some fun for once. For his entire life, Edwin felt that he'd had to live up to an impossible standard. Most PKs—preacher's kids—buckle under the pressure.

Reverend Jerome Batton, a good friend of the Lakes family who had a rather large ministry in East Orange, New Jersey, had three children. His youngest, a daughter, had a baby out of wedlock at sixteen. His only son, Jerome Jr., ended up in jail for assault with a deadly weapon when he shot his girlfriend when she attempted to leave him. Reverend Batton's oldest daughter dropped out of college and ended up married with two children, but none of his children followed in his footsteps—they rarely even made it to church.

Edwin was the model. He always did the right thing. He never gave himself a chance to make a mistake. As a teenager, Edwin stayed away from the kinds of things and people that would normally land normal teens in hot water. While other sixteen- and seventeen-year-olds were experimenting with weed and sex and clubbing, Edwin was studying and leading a youth ministry. He went right from high school into college and then into seminary—all with honors and distinction—as expected.

☆ ★ ☆

Once he stepped off the airplane in Miami, smelled the air and saw the palm trees, his world began to blossom. Miami in the mid-1990s was turning around—it had moved from the old-folks' retirement and Cuban refugee spot to the place for beautiful people, famous people, and rich people. This was before fashion designer Gianni Versace was shot to death in front of his home right on Ocean Drive. At that time it wasn't unusual to see Madonna at a club or strolling along Ocean Drive. Things were always happening. From Thursday to Sunday, Miami's South Beach turned into one big party. It was New York City, Times Square—only cleaner and more fun with the ocean and a clear sky as the backdrop. Edwin thought he had landed in heaven. He felt at home, strolling along the beach at night alone, listening to the waves and letting the moon light his path.

Edwin had found his center. Being in Miami around the beautiful people, beautiful beaches, and carefree lifestyle, he felt like he was sprouting wings. He felt like he was smelling the air for the first time. He felt like he could see colors he had never seen before. He was alive for the first time in his life.

Edwin got a small apartment on Collins Avenue, just around the corner from the beach and across the street from Hotel Leon. He had withdrawn enough money from his account to live on. He had been very good with his money, and his parents actually gave their blessing. They knew that Edwin needed this time away before he had to take on the Lakes family tradition—settle down, get married, have a couple of kids, and start his own ministry.

Edwin fell in love with Miami. And Edwin fell in love *in* Miami (or what he thought was love). They met at the Bed, a club/restaurant that was luxuriously made up with beds instead of tables and chairs. It was a trendy place with trendy people. Edwin didn't have many friends in general. And he had no friends at all in Miami. But he was determined to go to interesting places where he would meet interesting people. And on one particular night, "interesting" was an understatement.

As he sat at the bar, he struck up a conversation that led to the couple sharing a bed for dinner, then later a bed for other things. It was love at first sight. Electricity ran through Edwin's body with such a force that it scared him. He started to get warm around his ears. But he kept his composure, and he was expert at that. It was one of the first lessons he learned as a boy. As the son of a preacher, he could never be out of control.

Edwin was being groomed for the ministry before even he

knew it. But he still listened to his father's advice. "You must control your emotions, Edwin," his father would say. "You must always maintain control. People are depending on you to be their pillar, their rock."

For most of his life, Edwin maintained control. That's why he never really had a relationship that lasted. All of the women he dated complained that he was too cold and detached. His last girlfriend, Rebecca, who thought she would be Mrs. Pastor Lakes Jr., finally got fed up waiting for him to say "I love you." She had given him everything, but Edwin couldn't bring himself to open up. It was frustrating for her. And it was frustrating for him.

He'd made a promise to himself that he would never let another one go. Rebecca was special. She deserved more. Edwin knew that he had to have "it" in him before he could give "it" to someone else—whatever the "it" was. But he was determined to find out. Edwin was in Miami to get something to take back to the next one—the one who would eventually be Mrs. Pastor Lake Jr. She would get it all.

For the first time in his life, Edwin was living—really living. He was filling up his emotional tank.

He was dating, going to clubs and museums. He even went to a Miami Heat basketball game—this was before Shaq and Dwyane Wade and the all of the winning—but it was still exciting. He sampled all that Miami had to offer. He got to show off the physique that he spent some time crafting but never ever showed in public. The women in church could only imagine what was going on underneath those sharp, well-fitted suits, but the folks in Miami got to see the finely cut triceps, the chiseled back, and the hint of his six-pack as he took morning runs along the beach, followed by sit-ups and pull-ups at the workout bars on the beach. He would meet up with his newfound love for a smoothie at the Israeli-run health joint off Collins Avenue.

Edwin was living his dreams—a wild, crazy, frenetic love affair, which lasted for what seemed like the longest eight months in history. It was eight months of exploration. He had no idea how much light strokes of a tongue along his spine and the base of his behind would drive him crazy. No one had ever done that before. It was eight months of examination. It was eight months of being totally, unabashedly free.

One phone call at two in the afternoon as he was preparing to go Jet Skiing brought it all to an end.

"Ed-win . . ." He could tell it was his mother on the other end and she was crying.

"Edwin . . . you have to come home. Daddy had a massive heart attack. He died, Edwin. He died in the church office. . . ."

Edwin was numb. The senior Edwin Lakes wasn't just his father, he was Edwin's hero. His father was his teacher, his role model.

He held the phone close to his chest, trying to maintain his composure. Edwin, who always was prepared with the right thing to say, was at a loss for words. All he could muster was "I'll be right there, Mama. I'm coming right home."

Edwin started to pack up everything he had collected since he'd been in Miami. He'd purposely come with very little—a duffel bag with underwear, toiletries, two shirts, and a couple of pairs of shorts. He had planned on shopping in one of the best places in the world to shop—Miami. He was leaving with some fine linen slacks, a couple of dress shirts, jackets, and memories. Nice memories.

Edwin was taking the clothes and leaving the memories behind. He recalled the scripture about Lot and his wife. He would not be turned into a pillar of salt. He would have to be a pillar for the church and all that his father dreamed. Edwin would never turn back. He was moving forward. It was Edwin's time. Time to fill his father's size thirteens. Time to fulfill his destiny.

He had to leave Miami. Leave behind the beach, the fun. He had to leave everything—including the love he'd found, and that was tough. But he couldn't take it with him. The farewell would have been too painful, and he was already going through enough pain dealing with his father's death. Edwin didn't even want to think about saying good-bye. Good-byes only left open possibilities, and there were no possibilities where he was going. Edwin made a clean break, the break that was necessary for him to start his new life. No good-byes. No looking back.

Most of the congregation at Faith Baptist Church knew Edwin. They knew that he was away for further study—that was the story his parents told anyone who asked. While his parents didn't agree with his Miami frivolity, they knew he would be back. Edwin always knew he would be back, too— just not so soon.

10

"So, Heather, I hear you and your adorable hubby, Lorenzo, are still very frisky, how do you keep the magic alive?"

Heather Jones was a former child star who was one of the few child actors able to break out and succeed after puberty. There was Jodie Foster and Raven-Symoné and, of course, Ron Howard. But Heather Jones was on track to be bigger than all of them. She had a Grammy-winning CD and was starring in a new movie opposite The Rock. Her husband, Lorenzo Cohen, a star wide receiver for the San Francisco 49ers, had been named one of the sexiest athletes alive. Together, Heather and Lorenzo were also one of the hottest couples in the world.

Ritz had gotten some information from Chas, however, that would turn that picture perfect marriage into something out of *Kill Bill*. Ritz was itching to ask the questions, but she had to slow-walk it. Restraint was one of her strong suits. She was the consummate interview tease. Ritz knew she had to thread her needle carefully, butter Heather up, and help her let down her guard.

Ritz was known for plying her in-studio guests with food and liquor during the show. She would have the best champagne on ice with some lovely Tiffany glasses, courtesy of Mariah Carey. Mariah was the only artist who was smart enough to turn the tables on Ritz.

"Oooh! No fair!" Ritz said when she saw the gifts. "Don't think this is going to make me go easy on you!"

But it did. She and Mariah ended up talking and laughing and eating for two hours like old girlfriends. There was no mud-slinging, no juicy gossip, just girl talk. It was so anti-Ritz. And she vowed after that never to drink again on air.

So while her guests sipped on the strong stuff, Ritz had her glass filled with sparkling cider or diet ginger ale, poured before they came in.

Heather was starting on her second glass of champagne. Ritz had asked her about her new CD and movie during the first half hour, and now she was ready to move in for the kill. She was ready to talk about the things Ritz Harper was known for—the stuff her audience waited for every day.

"Let's talk about you and your man," Ritz started. "I hear lots of things about you two."

Heather blushed easily and squirmed a little in her seat.

"Well, what have you heard?" Heather said. "Wait. Don't answer that! Let's just say we're still very much in love."

"I heard that!" Ritz said. "You two are so much in love that you survived quite a strain on your relationship. I'm not sure if many couples could endure what you two have gone through and still be so tight and together."

Heather looked puzzled. She squirmed more and flashed a nervous smile as Ritz continued.

"Heather, girl. You must be a real special woman. Your man. Wow. I just don't know if I were in his shoes . . ."

Heather's milky complexion began to turn a shade of crimson that Ritz wasn't sure she had seen before. Was it anger or sheer embarrassment? It was certainly acknowledgment and recognition. Heather knew where Ritz was going even if the audience didn't know. Yet.

Heather sat frozen in her seat. She didn't speak.

"Woman to woman, Heather, how were you able to get through coming into a relationship with herpes?" Ritz said. "I know your husband didn't give it to you. But he accepted you anyway, married you, and you two are still happy. He clearly could have had any woman—any woman without herpes. But he chose you.

"There are thousands of women out there living with the shame of having a disease like herpes, and they don't know how to cope. Some don't know if they will ever have a relationship again. Next to HIV, herpes is about the worst thing you can think about having. There is no cure."

There was a long silence. And Ritz noticed Heather's bottom lip begin to quiver a little. Ritz gave a look to Aaron, who immediately put on what Ritz called her "sob story" music—

music she played very low under her unsuspecting guests to let the audience know that the guest was crying or about to cry.

"I—I didn't come on to talk about this," she said. The music grew a little louder. Ritz looked into Heather's watering eyes as compassionately as she could. She reached across the desk and grabbed Heather's hand and said, "I know and I'm sorry. I just thought your story could help some of the women listening to us today. But I understand if you don't want to talk." It was classic Ritz—the ability to be a real bitch and nasty, and at the exact same time be a soft, compassionate woman. It confused people. While a person was in the hot seat they knew they were being roasted, but it was almost like Ritz somehow hypnotized them. Once she locked them in her gaze, they were done. They would spill anything or give a reaction (like rage) that would keep the drama going. And don't let there be a little liquor in them.

Heather swallowed hard. "I contracted herpes in college from my college sweetheart. He was a star basketball player. He's in the NBA today."

"He is?" Ritz was practically salivating. This was better than she ever expected.

"Don't even bother asking, Ritz," Heather said. "I am not outing anyone. I'll talk about my business but no one else's. Really, this isn't any of *your* business. But perhaps I can help someone out there because I had no place to turn when it happened to me. And only by the grace of God did I meet someone like Lorenzo. I never thought I would have another relationship after my college boyfriend. I even thought because he gave me herpes that I was stuck with him so I put up with a lot that I shouldn't have."

"So you had herpes when you were on the last hit show?"

"Yes."

"Wow," Ritz said. "How did you have the confidence to wear that skimpy bathing suit? Weren't you afraid of an outbreak?"

"They do have medication to control the symptoms, and thank God I don't have outbreaks frequently. I have a very good gynecologist who has helped me through this ordeal tremendously."

"So what about kids?" Ritz said. "I hear herpes is dangerous for a baby. And how do you even, um, how do I put this, um, get to the point where you can have unprotected sex to produce a baby?"

"There are ways," Heather said. "And that's all I'll say about that. I would advise anyone who has herpes to check out the details with their doctor. Everyone is different and the disease affects different people differently. I have been very blessed."

"Yes, you have," said Ritz, turning the *People* magazine faceup to expose the couple on the cover, to rub it in even more. "Well, thank you so much for being so sweet and open. It was refreshing. You are now officially a part of the family here. We love you!"

Heather didn't say anything. She sat in her seat as Ritz went to a commercial break.

"It's five-fifty on the *Ritz Harper Excursion*. When we come back we'll take your calls. Stay tuned! You miss a minute, you miss a lot!"

When the "On Air" sign went dark, Heather got within inches of Ritz's face. "Did that feel good?" she hissed. "I hope you got everything you wanted." With that, Heather collected her bag and walked gracefully out of the room. Ritz looked at Aaron and shrugged.

"She was nice, huh?" Ritz said to Aaron, who broke out into laughter.

"You are a real trip, Ritz!"

"An excursion, love. An *excursion!*"

The phones were going crazy throughout the interview. Chas, who had been helping Jamie man the phones, jumped up from the studio and ran after Heather. Playing good cop, Chas caught her at the elevator and walked her out of the building, where her car was waiting. With his charm he convinced Heather that what happened with Ritz would not ruin her career.

"Heather, you have to know that there are so many women, maybe millions, who are suffering and thinking they are all alone," Chas said. "Now you are their role model and they know that there is hope because of you. Thank you for having the courage to be so honest."

Chas made Heather feel a little better. But deep down inside she knew that herpes would be a tough thing to overcome. She was on her way to being a big-time Hollywood leading lady. Herpes would make that a hard role to hold. It would be hard for an audience to see her in a love scene with a star like Will Smith and not think, "Ewww! Will, watch out! She has herpes!"

It was Chas who had booked Heather for the show. He knew her manager. It was Chas who slipped the herpes news to Ritz. He knew Heather's ex, the basketball player, who was a secret member of the Spy Room. And when he drank too much, he talked too much. Chas was someone everyone felt comfortable talking to. He was a very good listener.

These were the kinds of stories Ritz depended on Chas to deliver. After her Delilah Summers moment, there wasn't much else left in her repertoire. She needed help to take her thing to the next level.

"Chas, I know I have what it takes to be the very best this business has ever seen," said Ritz during one of their brainstorming Fridays over sushi while sitting at her kitchen island.

"Diva, you more than have what it takes," Chas reassured. "You just need a few more accessories. I promise I will take you to the top. I will take *us* to the top."

"I see what's out there, Chas. No one can touch me. But I also know I can never relax. I have to keep raising the bar, so none of those bitches out there can even get a leg on my shit. I want to raise this thing so high that they give up trying to catch me. Delilah was just a casualty—a necessary casualty. But we can take this even higher."

"No doubt. We will!"

Ritz needed Chas. She just didn't know how much. Chas was responsible for keeping Ritz at number one. For every single interview after Delilah that made the news or gossip pages, Chas, as promised, delivered the goods.

11

MIAMI, FLORIDA

It had been quite a few years since Ivan Richardson could remember having any real fun. Those were the days before he became a workaholic, the days before he was consumed with success, the days before his heart was broken. Ivan found satisfaction and fun in creating buildings from his imagination. He gained his pleasure from his latest projects.

As he sat in his gray Herman Miller Aeron chair at his large, art deco glass desk in his home office, Ivan thought about how he worked too much. He was becoming like so many of the men he read about—the kind of men who had everything and then suddenly dropped dead of a heart attack. He had read in *Jet* magazine about Glenn Cunningham, mayor of Jersey City, New Jersey—the first black mayor of Jersey City—who was at the top of his game and one day after coming home from riding his bike had a massive heart attack and died. The article talked about how he was in such great shape and how he was a workaholic.

"That won't be me!" Ivan muttered to himself as he took a sip of Georges Vesselle Grand Cru from his Waterford champagne glass. Ivan preferred the taste of champagne to wine in the afternoon. He especially liked high-end, smooth champagnes like Georges Vesselle. The bubbles made it feel less like alcohol. He then picked up the recent issue of *Ebony* magazine and smiled. The cover story was about the emergence of the megachurches. And on the cover was a familiar face.

Ivan was amazed by how so many blacks were flocking to church in record numbers and how so many ministers were becoming celebrities in their own right. There were pastors who had their own television shows, wore more bling than rappers, drove Bentleys, and lived in homes that looked like palaces—while those in their congregation went home to projects and tenements. To Ivan it was looking like a repeat of the days of Reverend Ike and Father Divine and Sweet Daddy Grace, those flamboyant ministers who would pimp off the poor in their communities, promising wealth and salvation.

Ivan's grandmother was a disciple of Sweet Daddy Grace. She was from Augusta, Georgia, and used to attend the House of Prayer religiously, a church that was packed with mostly women and effeminate men. There were too many rules—no makeup, no secular music, women couldn't wear pants. Ivan felt like a prisoner. He was a young boy on summer vacation but was held hostage with the fun literally wrung out of his life. He would gladly have attended school during the summer rather than suffer through this. Ivan was forced to sit on the hard wooden pews for what seemed like eighteen hours straight. His little legs, which dangled from the pews, often fell asleep, and he could barely walk when it was time to leave.

The only excitement came when Sweet Daddy Grace actually came to town. The House of Prayer was run by one of his many bishops. But when Sweet Daddy came to town, it was like the Fourth of July or more like Eastern Parkway in Brooklyn during the West Indian Day Parade. There would be dancing in the street, music (gospel, of course), baptizing, and lots of praise.

Ivan liked it when Sweet Daddy came to town. It would break up the monotony of what had become the bane of his existence. Sweet Daddy was a spectacle with his gregarious garb and his processed hair, worn long "the way Jesus did." Ivan liked to watch him.

But when he was not there, it was back to business as usual—the long, long, long, long services and the numerous women falling out with the "holy ghost." Ivan hated how the women, like Egyptian concubines, would fan the bishop. And he really hated when the big metal tubs would circulate around the church, taking the hard-earned money right out of the pockets of all of the unsuspecting worshippers. His grandmother was one of the biggest contributors. And all Ivan would think was "There goes my ice cream money."

Those summers spent in Georgia at the House of Prayer really made Ivan a cynic when it came to religion. He wasn't quite an atheist but he used to say to himself, "If these are the kinds of people who will be getting into heaven, I'll take my chances in hell!"

As Ivan got older, he started to search for the true meaning of life and God. He believed that there were a few ministers left who weren't out for their own selfish agenda. As Ivan stared at the *Ebony* cover, he reflected that Pastor Edwin Lakes Jr. seemed to be one of the good guys. He really did care about salvation and the souls of his congregants more than his bank account balance. He did preach the word. He was showing people that the true way to salvation didn't come through a Mercedes, a diamond, or a mansion, but more people were following the other, flamboyant preachers.

Pastor Lakes was becoming known because the younger generation—those in hip-hop—were flocking to his church. He bridged the two worlds of bling-bling ministries and down-home, word-based religion. He didn't drive a Bentley but he was fast becoming a star. He was handsome, handsome in the way actor Dennis Haysbert is handsome. Pastor Lakes was a full-size man, more than six foot three, with broad shoulders and a booming voice. From the pulpit he damn near looked like a black Zeus—larger than life with a singular command over his congregation.

Pastor Lakes also had a humility that softened what could have been a very intimidating visage. He was youthful—just over forty—but had a fatherly demeanor that made even

Elder Jenkins, who had been attending Faith Baptist Church in Harlem since she and Methuselah were kids, feel comfortable. Elder Jenkins hated change. She had had the same seat in the same pew for more than forty years and refused to move. And when the church decided to move from its small three-hundred-seat firebox to the cathedral-like three-thousand-seat space a few blocks away, she complained for months. But Elder Jenkins accepted Edwin as her pastor without a hitch.

Edwin Lakes had that way about him. In just a few short years after taking over Faith Baptist following the death of his father, he had built it into one of the fastest-growing churches in the nation.

Pastor Lakes earned that *Ebony* cover. And there he was with his stately mother at his left side, his beautiful and then pregnant wife, Patricia, at his right side and their little boy perched perfectly in his lap.

"You look great," Ivan said aloud to himself as he reclined slightly in his seat. "You certainly made it, my friend."

Ivan tossed the magazine across the table. It landed faceup.

Ivan, too, had made it. It had been nearly five years since he left his position as project manager at McKenzie & Braxton, one of the largest and most sought-after architect firms in Miami. Ivan was one of the most creative minds in the business. He found a way to incorporate his interior design skills into the actual architecture of his buildings. Ivan was an architectural genius, compared to Frank Lloyd Wright.

When Ivan left McKenzie & Braxton, many of their clients followed him. Within that first year, he had more business than he could handle. He was forced to take on a partner to pick up the load. He had envisioned himself being right where he was. But it felt empty. He didn't have anyone to share his success with—no children, no wife, no love.

As Ivan took another glance his old friend smiling on the cover of *Ebony*, having everything Ivan did not, he took another sip of his champagne and thought, "I guess you *can* have everything."

It was a coincidence that Ivan had had his assistant, Morgan, go out and get a copy of *Ebony*. One of Ivan's prized works—the Martin Luther King Memorial in Atlanta, Georgia—was featured in that issue, which happened to have the Lakes family on the cover. Coincidence? Or fate? Or maybe it was a sign. Divine intervention. The more Ivan stared at the picture of Edwin Lakes, the more Ivan got the notion that it was time to pay an old friend a visit.

Morgan, a tall woman in her forties with graying blond hair, was more than an assistant. She was Ivan's backbone. She had come with him from McKenzie & Braxton and knew the business inside out. Of all of the people there, Morgan was the most valuable, and he knew he needed her if his business was going to start off right. Ivan wanted Morgan. And Ivan got what Ivan wanted—one way or another.

"Morgan, I need you to arrange an open-ended ticket to New York and lodging," he said. "I'm not sure how long I'll be gone, but it is important business. Let's sit down after you have made the arrangements and put together a priority list of the things that need to be done in my absence."

She left to make the arrangements. Ivan rang her again.

"Morgan, make the flight for this evening, please," he said. "I'm leaving now to get some shopping done."

Ivan intended to have a good time and needed to have the right gear if he was going to be checking out the club scene. He picked the magazine up off the desk and tucked it under his arm. It would make good reading on the airplane ride to New York City. Ivan had spent the last four years building his business. It was time to get his groove back and maybe find a little religion along the way.

12

ON THE AIR

"Okay, Mark from Manhattan, the show is about over and I'm going to have to let you go," Ritz said in her best, exasperated I-can't-believe-this-nigga-is-still-talking voice.

"All I'm saying, Ritz, is that sometimes these hos need a pimp-slap from they man just so they know we care," Mark from Manhattan said. "Don't you remember your parents disciplining you out of love?"

"Uhhh! Mark, we have to go! I have to go and you most certainly *have* to go! I am unfortunately out of time. I love you for listening!" Ritz gave the signal and Snoop Dogg's "Drop It Like It's Hot" brought her show to a close. The song was old, but the beat was timeless and the message that her show would be eternally hot could never be lost.

As soon as the red "On Air" sign shut off, the studio

erupted into laughter. Everyone was laughing except Ritz. She was in one of her moods. Was it melancholy? Was she antsy? She couldn't put her finger on it. Jamie and Chas ignored her. They had learned to do that because recently they never knew what kind of shade Ritz would be throwing from day to day. She was turning into a real diva—attitude and all. Aaron and Chas and now Jamie worked hard to keep the ambience of the studio fun. Ritz could be so over the top that they needed to keep the balance.

"Yo, did you hear how serious that brother was about pimp-slapping his woman?" Aaron said. "Chas, maybe we can find his girl and bring her on the show. I bet he's full of shit. I bet we'll find out that he's the one getting pimp-slapped."

Chas could find anyone. Since he came on the show, there wasn't an interview Ritz couldn't have. Chas wasn't only well connected; he was so charming even straight men were attracted to him. He had that way about him. And since he had come to the station to work with Ritz, her show was doing better than anyone ever imagined.

Stations that had previously been ambivalent were now taking a second look. The *Ritz Harper Excursion* meant instant syndication success. It was heading toward full-out national syndication. Folks in Los Angeles and Miami wanted a piece of Ritz, who was enjoying her new lifestyle with its million-dollar-plus salary—which came on the heels of her hitting incentives every time her show came in the top three in the ratings.

Chas was proud. He was proud of his team.

He was particularly proud of Aaron and how he'd developed. When Chas came aboard, Aaron—a dark-skinned brother with curly hair and glasses, who if he wasn't so skinny could easily be mistaken for New York Jets running back Curtis Martin—was the board operator for Dr. Mark. He was on his way to being fired when Ritz moved to afternoons. Aaron didn't take shit from anyone and was fed up with what he deemed "the niggerish way" the station was being run. Management was fed up with him telling them how "niggerish" everything was. He was talented, but his anger and attitude overshadowed his talent at times. Aaron and Chas hit it off from the door and Chas schooled Aaron on how to play the game.

"Hey, what's your goal?" Chas asked. "To win, right? Well, my little brother, you have to know the rules and then learn how to play this game. Your first move is to lose the attitude."

Aaron did. And he became an integral part of the Ritz Harper team. He was even making a little name for himself with the on-air comments he was allowed to slip in from time to time. Ritz would use him when there was a lull during the five hours. She would harass him about his date the previous night and even talk to him about his foot fetish.

Once when she was interviewing sexy R&B ingenue Maria Marie, Ritz got the young singer to take off her shoes and show Aaron her feet. He went crazy and sucked on her big toe—and Maria Marie let him—on the air. It was classic, and it was these kinds of shenanigans that the *Ritz Harper Excursion* became known for.

Jamie, the intern, was sometimes disgusted by Aaron's antics. But most of the time she found him amusing. Secretly, Aaron was absolutely in love with Jamie. She, however, wouldn't give him a bit of attention.

The internship program was developed by Chas, who reached out to the broadcast and media departments of the local colleges. It was the first and only internship program at the station. Chas had Ritz announce a tryout for interns over the air and had them submit their bios and résumés. He personally interviewed the ones who seemed like winners. Chas put them through a grueling interview, but the real test came when they had to work with Ritz. During the five-hour show she would have them do everything from going across town to pick up her custom-made hair from Beverly Lugo Hair on Second Avenue, to going to Junior's in Brooklyn to satisfy her craving for strawberry cheese pie with amaretto chips. (At least she never made any of them walk to Junior's the way P. Diddy did on his *Making the Band* MTV reality show.)

Most of the interns ended up quitting in humiliation. The last one before Jamie was Brad, a senior at Hunter College. Ritz sent him to the store to get her some Kotex super tampons.

"They have to be Kotex!" Ritz said. "Don't come back here with no Tampax or Playtex. I don't wear those!"

Brad just didn't come back. Jamie was the next intern and she stuck it out. She passed the humiliating initiation period, which was Ritz's idea.

"You have to weed out those who really want to be down

from those who just want to hang around," she would say. Jamie really wanted to be down.

At twenty, she had a solid head on her shoulders and really knew what she wanted to do—she wanted to be in the business and, one day, on the air. Jamie wanted to learn every aspect of radio from the bottom up. On Ritz's show, Jamie was getting a top-drawer education.

Jamie, at five foot five, was a very pretty, brown-skinned girl with shoulder-length hair that she styled in a roller set that gave her a head full of bouncy curls. Jamie was serious and determined. She was on a mission. Chas saw that in her eyes from the first day he interviewed her. And she stuck close to Chas, learning all of his tricks and taking mental notes of all of his contacts and connections. And becoming more invaluable by the day.

Chas kept the show current. Ritz would be breaking news way before the *New York Post's* "Page Six" or the *Daily News'* "Rush & Molly" ever knew what was going on. They started listening to her show to fill their pages the next day. Chas would get a call from one of his sources all hours of the day and he would feed it to Ritz, who would have it over the air before he flipped his cell phone closed.

He was the big brother. He was the regulator. He was not only the producer, but he also kept everything and everyone in the studio on the same page.

They had turned into a little family—Ritz's dysfunctional, crazy, out-of-control family. Ritz needed the family atmosphere. Her world outside of the station was growing more and more strange. She couldn't really go out the way she used to because she was becoming so famous. The station had finally invested in promoting her, and her face was on bus ads, subways ads, and billboards around the city and throughout New York, New Jersey, and Connecticut. Ritz's face was becoming as well known as her voice. And the many television appearances she was making for some explosive interview or another were creating even more of a buzz around Ritz. There was even talk of a magazine-style show on VH-1.

Ritz wasn't comfortable in front of the camera. Her first love was being behind the mike and on the radio. She was at home there, but she was losing some of her inhibitions. For the first time, Ritz felt like she had people who had her back and that she could go out on a limb and there would be someone there to catch her if she stumbled or fell. Until now, Ritz had never trusted anyone to have her back. She couldn't. People always let her down. And honestly, she had never been the type of chick that people really wanted to look out for.

Ritz had only one true friend in the whole wide world—Tracee Remington. She was the one person who completely understood the madness that was Ritz. She knew the vulnerable Ritz, the sensitive Ritz, the soft Ritz that nobody—not even her studio family—knew. Hell, her own aunt and uncle didn't know that Ritz too well. But Tracee did.

Chas had glimpsed other sides of Ritz, but not as deeply as Tracee.

Ritz was slowly letting her guard down around Aaron and

Jamie. She was starting to trust, just a little. Tracee would caution Ritz not to be so skeptical.

"You don't trust people because you don't trust yourself," said Tracee. "That's all a reflection on you. You have to have faith and know that no one can do anything to you unless you let them. Everyone isn't out to get you. Everything happens in the fullness of time, and everything happens for a reason. You have to see the blessing in every situation, and even in your enemies you have to be able to see the good."

It was because of Tracee's advice that Ritz was open to Chas and let him into her world. Connecting with him was one of the best decisions Ritz had ever made.

Chas was always the last one out of the studio, constantly on the phone booking guests and setting up interviews. Most evenings after walking Ritz to her car, he would go back up to the station to make more phone calls and work on show strategy. Or Chas would go to a club, which was really more work than fun. Every now and then he would hang out with Ritz. Chas was the only one at the station who had been to her home.

Friday was supposed be their brainstorming night.

"Mr. Chas, are you free to work on the show tonight?" Ritz asked as they walked to her car on Friday. "Or do you have another date?"

"Look, don't be jealous," Chas said, poking Ritz playfully in the side. "I cannot help it that I am in high demand."

The comment stung Ritz a little but she never let on. She

was a little jealous of Chas's social life. Not that she would go out with as many men as he did or go to as many clubs. She just wanted to be asked. It seemed as if the more money she made, the more successful she became, the less attention she got from the opposite sex.

Chas wasn't trying to rub it in. He was simply trying to deflect. The truth was that he wasn't getting as much action as it appeared. He was hustling for the show. His "dates" were really contacts, opportunities for more exclusives. His "clubbing" was really spying to get more exclusives for the show. He liked Ritz and others to believe that he was some sort of magician who could pull stories for the show out of a hat, when in reality he was humping his behind to make sure that Ritz—and really his—star kept rising.

"You know what? I will cancel all plans tonight," Chas said. "It will be me and you. Let's order some Indian and pick it up on the way to your place. What's that spot on South Orange Avenue?"

"Neelam?" Ritz responded.

"Yeah, that one."

"Okay. I have a few ideas I want to run by you," Ritz said.

"I can't wait!" That's what Chas's mouth said, but he really didn't want any ideas from Ritz. He had all the ideas she would ever need. But he decided a long time ago to humor her.

He remembered reading in one of the many Machiavelli-style books that he seemed to devour whenever he got the chance that real power is in what is not seen. The truly powerful leave no fingerprints.

13

ON THE AIR

"This just in . . ." Ritz pressed the cough button to let Aaron know to play her news flash sound effect. "According this fax, LaFrance, hot young R&B diva and lead singer of the group Serendipity, has just had an abortion. This report comes directly from the Upper West Side clinic. Her wig and sunglasses didn't fool one observant clinic worker. We all know LaFrance as a super Christian. She is even releasing her solo gospel album next month. Stay tuned for more details."

Ritz pressed the cough button to let Aaron know to kill the news flash sound effect.

"Whoa!" Ritz said. "Can you believe this? I just saw her on the Grammys talking about 'the Lord' this and 'the Lord' that. Well! Isn't she a spokesperson for celibacy? Doesn't she claim to be a virgin? Well, maybe she had an immaculate conception. Maybe she just got rid of the second coming of Jesus. Oops! Did I say that?!

"I see the phone lines are lighting up. But we're out of time. We can pick this back up tomorrow. I love you for listening!"

☆ ★ ☆

Gradually, Jamie the intern began sticking around after Ritz's shift was over. She learned even more after the show, just being diligent in her work and not saying much. She didn't talk much, which made people feel really comfortable around her. It was another lesson learned from her father. In fact, Chas and Ritz sometimes forgot she was in the room.

"So, who are we going to ruin tomorrow?" Ritz asked sarcastically.

"You name the person and I'll make it happen, babycakes," Chas said. "Who do you want to take out next?"

"Hmmm. Whitney? Been there, done that! Michael Jackson? Done. Diana Ross? Damn, there's hardly anybody left worth taking out. Maybe we need a different approach. I don't know."

Jamie didn't react as she pretended to sort and file the faxes from the day.

"Nah. We have to stick with the formula. Ride the horse that brought us," Chas said.

"I'm getting a little tired of the drama, Chas. I mean, in the beginning it was fun turning over rocks and watching the critters squirm to get out of the line of fire. It was cool because I felt like we were taking down people who deserved it. Now it feels like we're just messing over people's lives."

"Ritz, baby, I know you're not getting soft," Chas said in a warning tone. "This isn't about messing over people's lives. Like you said, if they don't want folk in their business, they shouldn't be out there doing the things they're doing. You ain't making them cheat, lie, and steal. You're just telling on them when they do.

"Do you want to stay on top or what?"

"I do," Ritz said. "I know you're right. I've been talking to Tracee and she keeps reminding me about karma and how powerful words are. I'm just thinking."

"You do not get paid to think, baby. You get paid because of your ratings. You get paid to talk and talk about people. That's what you do. Now don't get all caught up in that Bible-thumping shit that Tracee is into. Look where it got her—in some damn retirement village. Focus. Don't get me wrong. I love Tracee. No disrespect. But when Miss Thing breezes into town, I have a few words for her. She's trying to mess this up."

"I know. I know. But—"

"But nothing! I can't believe we're having this conversation. Ritz Harper! You better go home and get some sleep and get your head together. In fact, I'll walk you out to your car. We need some fresh air."

Ritz looked over at Jamie, who was still pretending to sort faxes.

"Don't work too hard, Jamie," Ritz said. "You aren't getting any overtime."

Jamie finally looked up and smiled. "Overtime? I haven't seen a paycheck!"

"Oh, yeah. You are still an intern." Ritz winked. "You get home safely. We'll see you tomorrow."

"I'll just finish up. See you guys tomorrow."

"Bye, baby girl," Chas said, then turning to Ritz. "You wearing that old rag again? We're going to have to go shopping this weekend for a new fur. You've got to be runway ready, baby. Runway ready!"

As Ritz and Chas headed out of the studio and toward the elevators, Jamie pulled out her Nextel BlackBerry mobile phone. There were four voice-mail messages and a half dozen e-mails. Jamie kept her phone turned off while she was working. She wanted to give the appearance that she was giving Ritz and the show her undivided attention. And she was.

But Jamie had a recent distraction. His name was Derek. She'd met him on the train a few weeks before. She was attracted to his tough, thuggish exterior. He was attracted to her ass, which he got to look at a lot as they stood for nearly forty minutes on the crowded Number 4 train to the Bronx.

Jamie had been raised in a nice, upper-middle-class (on the edge of wealthy) home in suburban Westchester. She came from a nice, moral home and lived on a tree-lined street. But she always had a secret attraction to boys from the other side of the tracks. Jamie never brought them home and rarely introduced them to any of her neighborhood friends. But bad boys were Jamie's secret weakness.

Derek was twenty-seven, had his own place, drove a concrete-white Navigator with twenty-four-inch chromes. And it was always clean. His closet was filled with new but understated gear. He didn't wear jewelry but could certainly afford to. He recognized that his success was attributed to his ability to fly under the radar. Derek was a student of the game. He watched a lot of films like *Hoodlum, Lansky, Once Upon a Time in America*, and of course the *Godfather* trilogy. Derek was smart enough to learn from others' mistakes, and the one lesson he learned as a black man in his game was to not look typical.

He didn't wear white Ts or hoodies or fitted hats. He was fly-guy casual—Cavalli jeans, Gucci tie-ups. His only jewelry was a Panerai watch with a plain black Toscana strap, no ice. He was clean cut, low key, and spoke in low tones. He was going to learn from his brother's mistakes and keep his business and his personal life very, very separate. He would roll with very few "soldiers" and had no real close friends.

His new home was miles away from where he did his business, and he made sure few in his business knew where he lived.

"You don't eat where you shit—even animals understand that," said Derek's brother, Jayrod, who had good advice that he himself never followed. Not too many in the "street pharmacy" business followed the rules. Their egos and arrogance usually got the best of them. Derek was a good student.

Unlike his brother and others he grew up with, Derek also recognized that doing business with a certain ilk will get you killed or in jail. His clientele was high-end—folks in the music industry, from executives to some of the elite stars. People with something to lose. He also serviced the film industry, from producers and set designers to even an Emmy-winning actress. His brother, Jayrod, gave him his first connection in the music industry through platinum-selling rapper Big Fun, who got his weekly supply of haze delivered in the bottom of a case of Cristal. Big Fun smoked more weed than Snoop. It was even part of the rider in his contract—the list of demands that artists give to promoters when doing concerts. That list usually included FIJI Water, Skittles, or whatever the artist liked to enjoy in his dressing room before appearing on stage. Big Fun's rider always included an ounce of purple haze and, if he was on the West Coast, an ounce of Cali Cush. Jayrod was his supplier. When he got sent upstate, little brother Derek took over.

Big Fun liked Derek's style, his low-key demeanor, so much that he hooked him up with some of his other friends. And when Big Fun crossed over into movies, Derek crossed over with him, making his own connections. Derek's business grew to five times the size of his brother's. And no one ever knew—not even Jayrod. Derek didn't talk much and he certainly never bragged.

He did his dirt, though. He had his grimy moments. And that was what attracted Jamie. She could see through the polos and the khakis. She could smell the dirt and the success commingling the way funk and cologne does on some people to make a powerful, intoxicating aroma.

Jamie and Derek exchanged phone numbers on the Number 4 train. Their meeting would not have ever happened under normal circumstances. Derek, who was having a stash box installed in his Navigator big enough to hold a pound and a 9mm, was going over the final details with the installer at an underground body shop in Spanish Harlem when he happened to look at his watch.

"Oh, shit!" he said to no one in particular. "Chico, if you have any questions, hit me on my cell. I have to run."

Derek had about fifteen minutes to get to Midtown for an appointment. He prided himself on never being late. He wouldn't be able to get a cab to get there on time, so he hopped on the Number 4 train. Derek hadn't taken the train since high school. But he didn't forget which line could get him to his destination the fastest. He had no idea that the fateful ride would give him a chance to meet another new contact: Jamie.

Jamie built up her nerve to talk to him the first stop after he got on. She didn't want to risk his getting off at the next stop without getting his number so she boldly approached him.

"You seem like you have a lot on your mind," she said coyly.

"Huh?" said Derek, a little startled, but he recovered quickly. "Right now, it's just you."

Jamie smiled. She liked him instantly because even with that line, he came off as genuine. Maybe that was another reason why Ritz Harper had grown to depend on Jamie so much. Jamie was their in-studio lie detector. When a guest was in the studio and Ritz asked a particularly sticky question, she would often turn to see if Jamie had a reaction.

While Ritz prided herself on her ability to interpret body language, which she had learned in college, Jamie had a real sixth sense about people that they could never teach in school.

She knew Derek was a hustler. She knew that he was probably even dangerous. But she knew something else. She knew she liked him.

They exchanged numbers. He called first because he knew that was the proper thing to do. They talked a few times after their meeting on the train and then set up their first date.

He invited her to go shopping—far from the typical first date.

"I just got this new apartment a couple of months ago, but I've been working so much that I haven't had time to decorate. Maybe you can help me pick out some things. I think I need a lady's touch."

"You seem like you have very good taste. I'm honored," Jamie said. "What do you do that keeps you so busy, anyway?"

"I do sales," he said. "I work on commission."

"Sales, huh?" Jamie said to herself. There was something about the way Derek said it made her not pursue it further.

Jamie took Derek to an eclectic store on Seventh Avenue near Sixteenth Street. They had a large, stylish selection—it was Chelsea, after all. Jamie picked out a couple of prints that were earth tones—not too masculine but definitely not feminine. The pillows she selected were large and Asian-styled. Derek smiled.

"You haven't even seen my bed and you picked out something that's perfect for it," he said.

"So, now I *have* to see this bed myself to see if you're lying." But she knew he wasn't lying.

"You will," he said. "Tonight."

Tonight? She felt her stomach flutter uncontrollably thinking about it as they moved to the rug section of the store. She picked out a sisal rug with green and brown trim. After they finished shopping, he asked her if she liked Chinese food.

"Of course!" she said. "Who doesn't like Chinese?"

"Let's get takeout," he said. "I want to see how these pillows really look on my bed."

They caught a cab back to his place. Carrying the area rug and two pillows, they finally arrived at Derek's apartment near the Riverdale section of the Bronx. It was a beautiful space. Empty, but beautiful.

She held the bag of Chinese food while he laid the rug down in the empty living room. He lit three large candles and put the pillows down and grabbed two square plates that he had never used. He turned on his Bang and Olufsen BeoSound 9000 with the six-CD changer. Derek figured he could spend a little money inside his home without attracting too much attention. To Jamie's surprise, vintage Luther started to play.

"I was expecting DMX," Jamie said to herself. She was impressed.

That night was one of the most romantic Jamie had ever experienced. When they finished eating, Derek showed her around the place. It was a quick tour—two bedrooms, one bathroom, a European-style kitchen, and a large living room. He lived in a renovated prewar building on the third floor. The place had hardwood parquet floors and crown molding.

"Salesman, huh? What is he *really* selling?" Jamie wondered as she looked around. But she knew the answer to that, too.

He showed her the first bedroom, which was the first room along the hallway after the kitchen.

"I plan on making this my office," Derek said.

He showed her the next room, the bathroom, which was white with white hexagonal tiles.

"He definitely needs my touch," Jamie thought as she plotted taking him to Bed Bath & Beyond to get some colorful bathroom accessories. A few years ago she had also eyed a wonderful teak bathmat in a Hold Everything catalog that would fit in nicely.

Then he led her to his bedroom.

"This is where it all happens," he said jokingly.

"What? Sleep?" said Jamie, laughing.

"Exactly!" he said with a sheepish grin.

"Yeah, right!" Jamie thought, but didn't say anything. "He's got the nerve to be modest about his shit, too? I like that."

There was nothing in his bedroom but a dark cherry platform bed and matching nightstands and lamps. But his bedding was impeccable. He had powder blue sheets.

"Is that six-hundred-thread-count Egyptian cotton?" she wondered.

And he had a huge white down comforter that looked like fifty cumulus clouds sitting on his bed. He didn't have a television or a radio or anything else in the room. Just the beautiful bed, nightstands, and lamps.

"I guess this is *really* where it all happens," she thought.

Jamie wanted to stay the night but thought it wouldn't be a good idea.

"Who gives a fuck about a good idea?" Jamie thought. She was having an internal battle between her good senses and her loins, which were beginning to ache slightly for no particular reason.

The scent of Derek's Chrome cologne—which was so light she could barely smell it but what she could take in smelled so good that she wanted to bury her face in his neck to get more—was starting to work on her. That and his body. Derek was about five foot ten and built like a martial artist. Even in his khakis and polo she could make out the fine lines of definition. And when he pushed up the sleeve of his shirt to disclose the most beautiful forearms she had ever seen, she thought she would lose her mind. His forearms looked like chiseled wood carvings.

He kept his reddish brown hair closely cropped, and his goatee was well groomed—but not too well groomed. Jamie thought some guys went too damn far clipping and shaping their facial hair (like that Ginuwine).

"Hey, girl," Derek said. "Ready to go?"

"Wait a damn minute," she thought. "He is *too* smooth—ushering me out, knowing full well that will only make me stay. He's good."

Instead of answering him, Jamie moved right up to within inches of his face, slowly grabbed the back of his head, and kissed him. It was as if he expected it because his mouth was ready. He took the tip of his tongue and slowly circled hers, pulling back to suck lightly on the tip of hers. He nestled her bottom lip between his and pulled until her mouth opened and he plunged in gently with his tongue.

Jamie thought her coochie was going to fall right out from between her legs. It was on fire. Jamie never imagined a kiss would make her feel like that. His kiss was light and his tongue was warm. He put his arms around her waist and leaned in on the kiss.

"I better go now" came out of Jamie's mouth, but her coochie was screaming "You have got to be fucking kidding!"

"Okay," he said, letting her slide out of his arms. "I'll call you."

She somehow found herself at the front door. Her damn

feet, working in cahoots with her brain, had betrayed the rest of her body once again.

"Girl, make sure you call me so that I know you got home safely," he said. "And here." He pressed a crisp fifty-dollar bill into her hand. "This is for the car service."

Jamie didn't front, either. On her internship stipend of nothing she didn't really have the money to be taking a car service. Her parents still gave her an allowance, but she didn't have it like that. She smiled and stopped herself from kissing him good-bye.

"If I go back there I'll definitely not leave," she thought to herself as she walked down the stairs to the street.

Jamie called him when she got home and every day after that.

14

Ivan opened the door to his hotel room and was pleased with his clean, modern surroundings. He had stayed at several upscale hotels during his trips to New York—from the Plaza and the Waldorf-Astoria to the Four Seasons. He hated old carpet and what he decided was the gaudy and stuffy decor of both the Plaza and the Waldorf. He also hated the heavy ornate drapes that made all the rooms he checked into seem heavy and dark. It was as if the old furnishings had absorbed the sad feelings of all the guests throughout the years.

The Four Seasons on East Fifty-seventh Street was perfect, but the five-hundred-dollar-a-night rate for the kind of room he wanted was too steep even for Ivan's fat pockets. He didn't know how long he was actually going to stay in Manhattan, and throwing away that kind of money went against his frugal grain. Watching his grandmother work so hard and die with nothing made him keep a careful eye on his finances.

Ivan settled on an out-of-the-way spot in SoHo. Discreet, reasonable, and trendy. His room boasted a small balcony. There was only room for him to stand out there alone, but when the French doors were open and he pushed back the curtains, it provided a wonderful view and made his room come to life with the craziness of New York City. It felt more like a small apartment than a musty old hotel room.

Ivan opened his suitcase on the couch facing his bed at the other end of the room and began hanging up his clothes. He immediately realized that he had forgotten to pack clothes to work out in. Ivan was part of the beautiful-people pack. In the midst of his heavy work schedule, he made sure every day to take at least an hour and half to either get in a run or find a gym and a treadmill. He also lifted weights and was proud that under his Brooks Brothers suits was a body to die for.

He knew he would be staying in New York long enough that he would need to work out. Ivan decided he would finish unpacking later. It was already three in the afternoon, and he needed to buy some sneakers and some workout gear. He headed down Eighth Street off of Sixth Avenue in the Village in search of a sneaker store. He decided that running would be a big part of his workout. He checked out the hotel gym; the equipment left a lot to be desired. He scoped out Washington Square Park and the surrounding areas and decided that it looked like a decent place to run.

Ivan was in New York to have fun. It was Miami-squared

in terms of opportunity and nightlife. His last visit to New York taught him how wild things could be. While he wasn't looking for wild, he was definitely looking for excitement. As he headed past West Fourth Street and the cage that was filling up with ballers, he was bombarded with flyers for a "hot" party or the best place for a piercing or tattoo.

After walking about three blocks, Ivan finally found a store with a huge selection of running shoes. The salesman asked Ivan to take a seat. Ivan loved to shop. He got a euphoric feeling whenever he was doing it. That coupled with R. Kelly's "Happy People" blaring from the sound system put a real bounce in his late afternoon. The salesman returned and Ivan held up the Nike running shoe he wanted and asked for a size twelve.

The store had on a radio station, not the normal Musak or XM Radio. The woman's voice on the radio was intoxicating. He had no idea who she was, but it sounded like she was loving life and loving what she was doing. Ivan decided that he was exactly where he needed to be—New York City. The Big Apple. Land of dreams. He was thirty-four years old, relatively wealthy, and out of touch with his youth. He was tired of wondering where P. Diddy, who was pushing forty, found the energy to party as much as he did. He ran up to the register and asked for a pen.

He heard the lady with the intoxicating voice talk about a party the next evening at Club Red that she was hosting. It sounded like the spot. Ivan took the address and knew that tomorrow would be the first night of getting back his groove.

"That'll be $134.96, sir," the store cashier said. "Would you like a pair of socks to go with those?"

"In fact, I'll take five pair," Ivan said. "And please tell me what station we're listening to."

"Oh, that's WHOT, Hot-9—99.9," the cashier responded while handing Ivan back his platinum AMEX.

"Who's that lady talking?"

"You must not be from around here." The cashier got sassy. "That's Ritz Harper! She's off the hook. They call her the Queen of New York. She has the lowdown on everybody."

Ritz was in the middle of a great blind item about a movie star whose wife caught him in their swimming pool banging some TV magazine host. She said she had to go to commercial break but would have more details when she came back. Ivan found himself hooked. He was disappointed that he wouldn't be hearing the rest. But he had to get back and get prepared for tomorrow. He needed his beauty sleep.

15

Chas got to the club around midnight. He liked to get there before Ritz to scope out the spot. Since her heightened fame, Ritz also liked Chas to check the exits and make sure that everyone in her surroundings looked copasetic. He often thought she was paranoid, but he would never let Ritz know that he thought she was overreacting.

Ritz was set to arrive around midnight to host a bash at Club Red. Chas was certain that she would be late; it was getting more and more difficult to get her to come to appearances. She was feeling herself.

"What stars still have to make appearances?" she would complain.

"Ritz, they're apart of your contract," Chas would reason. "Besides, it's the one time when you get to be with your people and they get to see you."

"Fuck that!" Ritz said. "They don't need to see me. Those thirsty bastards will tune in whether I'm hosting a party or not. In my next deal, I'm not doing any more appearances unless it's on my very own television show!"

While Ritz hated doing appearances, she loved the money. She could pocket anywhere from two thousand to ten thousand in cash depending on the event. And while Chas was always there, Ritz never shared a dime with him. He never let show that he minded her stinginess, but he did.

But it was Ritz who people showed up to see. She was the star attraction. She *was* the star—dressed to impress in Rock & Republic jeans, a beaded Luca Luca top, Ferragamo sandals, and lots of hair. Chas knew his role and his place.

Club Red was packed with people waiting in anticipation for the arrival of "the diva."

Everyone looked fabulous—including Chas. He always looked fabulous. He took his own advice on always being "runway ready." He had on a new Ryan Kelly shirt, simple black slacks—no need to overdo it there—and black Gucci loafers. He also had on a black Gucci watch, which you had to look at real hard to notice that it was Gucci. Chas liked that.

"Ritz thinks she's a diva," Chas thought. "But she could never be a real diva. That takes some of the subtleties she has yet to master. If she ever will."

Chas felt at home in the club. He loved when Ritz had appearances at clubs. He loved the energy of the people, the music, the lighting. It was like being in a dream. Lately it was also fodder for the show. He would get to the club and pick up some gossip. There would always be a few celebrities at the club. When they drank too much, someone was bound to do something that would be worthy of a blind item, at the very least. During Ritz's last appearance, Majita, Tracee's former artist, was looking suspiciously skinny and jittery.

Chas took his post near the bar and began scanning the dance floor and VIP section for anyone famous. All he could see were shapes as the strobe and spotlights moved around the floor. But one figure stood out. Perhaps it was because it was a solo figure dancing its ass off all alone. Perhaps it was the striking physique that was so well defined that every move looked like music itself.

When the song was over, the man walked over to the bar where Chas stood, sipping on a glass of Martell XO or Louis the XIII Cognac—two hundred dollars a snifter. Chas didn't want to get drunk; he just wanted a nice, smooth buzz.

"Hello, stranger," said Chas, turning up his charm more notches than should be legal.

"Chas?!" the man said, sweat dripping from his face. "What are you doing here?! Don't let me find out you're stalking me." Ivan gave Chas a warm but masculine hug as the two laughed.

"You wish I was stalking you!" Chas said, shouting over the music. "When did you get town? And what happened? Why didn't we ever keep in touch?"

"You should be asking yourself that question," Ivan said. "The phone rings both ways, last I looked."

"Well, you know how I feel about going both ways," Chas said, leaning in to Ivan's ear and then rearing back to let out a howl of infectious laughter.

"You are still crazy," Ivan said. "Hey, you want to get out of here and catch up?"

"I have to wait for my girl to show up," Chas said. "She's hosting the party."

"Ritz Harper? That's your girl?"

"More than that. I produce her show!"

"Get out of here!" said Ivan. "I am only here tonight because I heard her on the radio earlier. I like that lady. She is something else!"

"Yes, she is! Yes, she is," Chas said. "You still never told me what you're doing in the city."

"Well, I thought it was time for me to have some fun and put a little spice in my life. I have an old friend here, too, who I haven't seen in a while. I am thinking about checking him out."

"Checking *him* out?" Chas asked. "Hmm. You trying to make me jealous?"

"Oh, stop! It's kind of complicated."

"I specialize in complicated," Chas said. "Ritz better hurry up, so you and I can really catch up."

Ritz did finally breeze in around one-thirty in the morning after which Chas and Ivan left the club and did a little more than catch up.

Tracee hired a limo to take her to the Orlando International Airport for her four o'clock flight. She filled up her iPod with sermons by Pastor Edwin Lakes, Creflo Dollar, Joel Osteen, and a bunch of gospel music.

She decided to take a sauna and then get ready for the trip. Tracee sat in her sauna and opened her Bible to the book of James. It was her favorite book, and she began her day reading the short but powerful five chapters. She was one of the few people in Florida with a sauna. Hot tubs were big. Everyone seemed to have a swimming pool. But saunas in Florida seemed almost redundant when temperatures were in the eighties in the winter and over a hundred degrees in the summer.

Tracee, who was from New Jersey, discovered the healing power of saunas and became addicted. She had a portable one in her Manhattan loft and decided to build one in her huge bathroom in her Winter Garden home. Her sauna could seat three but no one had shared that space with Tracee—not yet. She liked to sprinkle a little eucalyptus, peppermint, or grapefruit oil on the hot rocks before pouring distilled water over them, releasing a fragrant steam that seemed to pierce her bones. She couldn't take more than twenty minutes at a time. But that's all Tracee needed to get her head straight for the day. With each breath of steam she inhaled, she was building up her immune system and her defenses.

"This is like spiritual vitamin C," she thought with a chuckle. "I better stay in here an extra ten minutes just to be sure."

Tracee didn't need a lot of time to get ready. She could pack light because she still had her Manhattan loft where she kept some clothes. Whatever she didn't have, she would buy. She had more money than she could ever imagine spending.

She would have to buy something to go with Ritz to the Grammys. This was a big time in Ritz's life, and Tracee wanted to be there for her. The last conversation they had, Ritz sounded funny. She needed to talk—not on the phone. The phone was phony conversation. There was a study done that showed that people could be easily deceived over the phone. Relationships between people that started on the phone rarely lasted, and if they did, they were rarely real. There's nothing like looking into a person's eyes and seeing where they are really coming from, what is really on their mind.

Tracee looked forward to looking into Ritz's eyes. Over the

last several months Tracee had been dropping kernels of truth on her friend. But she really wanted to get in there and talk to her about her spirit, about her life. Tracee had changed so much. And as much as Ritz had to share, Tracee had just as much to share, too. She was compelled to, before it was too late. There were things Ritz had to come to grips with, had to deal with, had to know.

☆　　★　　☆

For nearly five years, Tracee Remington rode the wave of success as artist after artist on her label sold millions and millions of records and won Grammys and MTV Music Awards and People's Choice Awards. Her label became almost a conveyor belt of platinum CDs. But her artists didn't have longevity. As soon as they hit, it seemed like they dropped off just as quickly.

Christopher "Hardcore" Harris seemed to be on a different path—one leading toward longevity. His first CD sold more than three million copies. His second one sold that many in just the first month.

Tracee liked Hardcore. She got to know him during a month-long promotional tour through the Midwest and West Coast. She discovered that his thug act was just an act. He rose to fame as so many did on a harsh street life that included being a former drug dealer—which wasn't new. He claimed to be a protégé of Tom Mickens aka Tony Montana from the Merrick Boulevard area in Queens. That was big time. But it was a big time or image play. Unlike rappers like 50 Cent, who bragged about being shot, Hardcore talked about the "niggas he shot." He even alluded to actually killing someone. That set him apart. He had a persona that people didn't cross. He didn't wear a bulletproof vest, didn't travel with an entourage; he had a steely glare and a deep voice that he didn't use often, and he rarely smiled. His image worked like a charm. Inside, however, he was quite the opposite.

That image was completely manufactured. He practiced the icy stare and didn't talk much because he was constantly talking to himself inside his head trying not to be overwhelmed by everything that was happening.

Tracee got to see the vulnerable side of Hardcore, and she even let down her guard a bit—which she never did with her artists.

Around the fourth stop on their West Coast tour, Tracee and Hardcore had a heart-to-heart while on an hour-and-half drive to an appearance at a radio station in Las Vegas.

"Tracee, I'm glad you're on the road with me," Hardcore said.

Tracee wished that she could say the same. She couldn't. It wasn't him. She just hated being on the road. But she didn't want to insult him. He was making an attempt to be deep. Hardcore was thirty-two, playing tough and pretending to be in his twenties.

"I'm tired, Core," she said. "I hate being on the road. But I must say, the company isn't half bad."

Hardcore smiled. He had beautiful teeth that few rarely got to see. "I hear you. I never expected there to be this much attention on me. I mean, I wanted to be a big hit, but this is ridiculous."

"It's only the beginning, so you better get used to it," Tracee said.

Hardcore stared out of the window and didn't respond.

They arrived at the radio station, a rundown studio in the middle of the desert. Hardcore gave his interview, which amounted to four or five words. He dropped a promo that the station would be using ad nauseum, then he and Tracee hit the road back to Los Angeles.

"What comes next?"

"Well, we have five more radio stations to hit and then you have a couple of club dates, an appearance on Jimmy Kimmel, and then back home to cut your next CD."

"No, I mean what happens next—after the fame and money?"

It was a question Tracee had never been asked, and she had no answers.

"I've been reading a lot of financial books—David Bach, Suze Orman, even Napoleon Hill—and they talk about exit strategies and plans," Hardcore said. "I don't have an exit strategy or a plan. After I sell all of these CDs and collect all these checks, then what?"

"I don't know, Core. That's a damn good question."

"Could I just walk away?"

"Why would you want to? I mean, the sky's the limit for

you. You can be the biggest rapper ever—the biggest performer ever. You can break records."

"And then what? I already don't have privacy. I can't go anywhere or do anything without being mobbed. People spying on me, even wanting to kill me."

Tracee spent so much time crafting and maintaining images and playing traffic cop for artists that she never stopped to consider the consequences of their success or the images she helped to foster. There was a reason why so many artists from Billie Holiday to Elvis, Janis Joplin to Jimi Hendrix, got strung out on drugs and ended up basically killing themselves. Tupac's and Biggie's murders didn't happen in a vacuum, nor were they coincidences. Groundwork was laid that led up to them. Was Hardcore on the same path?

As they pulled in front of the Doubletree Hotel in Los Angeles, Core got out and extended his hand like a perfect gentleman and led Tracee out of the limo. Tracee smiled and walked toward the entrance of the hotel where a beautiful waterfall splashed into an exotic koi pond.

"That's what I'm talking about," Hardcore said, looking at the pond. "I want to have shit like this in my home."

"In another two weeks you will be getting your first real royalty check and you can buy all the fish you want!"

In the music world, the illusion of money supersedes the reality. Most artists get little more than a per diem—enough for daily meals, car service—and an advance that many blow in the first few days on perishables like cars and jewelry. The real money doesn't come until *after* the first hit CD.

"Yo, I'm real excited about that," he said. "I'll be able to buy my first home. And you don't have to worry about seeing my ass on *Cribs*, either. Hell no! I don't want no niggas knowing how I'm really living."

"Core, I have got to say, you have come a long way! I'm proud of you."

"Thanks, Tracee, for just being real with me all the time."

"No problem!" Tracee said. "You know how I do." They both laughed, and Hardcore gave Tracee a big hug and thanked her again.

Tracee and Hardcore walked to the elevator laughing at the condition of the radio station they just left. As the elevator door opened, Hardcore grabbed Tracee's hand.

"Not so fast," he said. "I have a gift for you."

He reached into his bag and pulled out a box. Tracee was a little surprised. Most of these artists spent their money on dumb stuff like weed or liquor or on impressing their entourage. And when it came to women, if they weren't stripping or giving head, they wouldn't be getting a dime. But here he was giving her a box.

"Open it!" he said like an excited kid. "It's not much. I just want you to know how much I appreciate everything you've done for me."

Tracee opened the card first. It simply read: "Thank you! Christopher Harris." Then Tracee opened the box to find a state-of-the-art Nike heart monitor and MP3 player all in one. It was something she would have never thought to get herself, and she was impressed at how well Christopher had listened to her. She couldn't remember them ever really talking about her love of working out but she must have.

"Thank you, Core," Tracee said. "Thank you so much! I really do need this."

"Cool!" he said. "Glad you like it. I'll talk to you tomorrow. Have a great night's sleep."

"You, too!" Tracee said as she got into the elevator.

"He's a good guy," Tracee thought. "Finally, one of these artists might actually make it. I think Hardcore's going places."

But thanks to Ritz Harper, the only place Hardcore was going was down in flames.

A rapper can be a criminal, a crackhead, a drug dealer, even a murderer, but the one thing that can absolutely kill a rap career is being outed as gay. That was hard to overcome.

ON THE AIR

"From what I hear . . . Hardcore likes it hard in the core," Ritz said during the final hour of the show. She sometimes saved some of her juiciest tidbits until the end, forcing her audience through the entire five hours to get to the real dirt.

"Okay? To put it more plainly—the only thing hard about Hardcore is the men he enjoys. Shut *up*!"

Aaron played the sound effect of a gay man howling "Ooooooh, how you doin'?!" on cue, and everyone in the studio let out a collective *Ooooooh!*

"No, Ritz, nooooooo!" Tracee screamed her head off in her

office, where she was listening to the interview. "Oh, shit! Oh, shit! Shit! Shit!"

This was rap. Much of Hardcore's success came because he had, until this point, lived up to his name. He was tough. And he carried himself that way. He dared someone to test him and no one did. No one except Ritz Harper.

"Word on the street has it that Hardcore only gets really hardcore when around some buff beefcake in a special club," Ritz continued like a pit bull clamped down on a piece of meat. "And word has it he's not the pitcher, but the *catcher* . . . if you know what I mean."

Tracee had never once asked Ritz not to go there with one of her artists. She would never get in the way of her girl doing her thing. Ritz never even connected the dots she was drawing back to her friend—never put two and two together that ruining Hardcore might somehow affect Tracee, too. Ritz was in a trance when she was on the air. She was another person in another place. Tracee didn't like the on-air Ritz very much. But she understood her and even respected her gangster—her desire to expose the liars, the cheats, the crooks, the bullshitters.

Tracee loved her off-air friend to pieces. But as she sat in her big chair, behind her big desk in her big corner office, she began to contemplate her career. Her role in the music business was solely to cover up and appease. She was not just babysitting, she was enabling, and she wasn't making a difference. At least Ritz thought she was providing a public service. And in many ways she was—uncovering the truth (albeit in a sordid way).

Following Ritz's bomb drop, Hardcore's third CD barely reached gold, and he was officially done. So was Tracee, but it took a few more incidents to seal it for her.

One evening she was at an appearance with one of her female rap artists at Club New York on the West Side. Tracee didn't remember how or why, but there was something about a shoe being stepped on and some finger-pointing that led to some weave-pulling. Before she knew it, she was in the middle of a melee, looking for an exit, while pulling her artist by the arm. The cops came and Tracee found herself with a split lip; her artist had a black eye. And Tracee had had enough.

"I can't do this shit anymore!" Tracee said to no one in particular.

The cops asked her if she wanted to press charges. But Tracee made a decision right then that all she wanted was out. She wouldn't press charges, she would press on. She had had enough. Enough of the weed-filled limo rides to appearances and award shows. Enough watching the overindulgence in the E-pills, the coke and the gratuitous sex. Enough of the groupies and the fear of rape charges. Enough of getting grown people to be responsible enough to show up for booked dates like for the *Regis & Kelly* show (which on more than one occasion one of her artists completely blew off). Enough watching these same grown people blow fortunes on jewelry and drugs, cars and toys—things that they couldn't even sell if they got in a bind and needed money. Tracee was dead tired of the Mr.-Bojangles-Nigga-Samboing-Stepin-Fetchit-pimps-and-hos cartoon that rap music—hell, all music—had become and how more and more young girls preferred to be video hos than video producers, writers, and teachers.

Tracee was tired of the industry and her "bosses." They had put her in charge of the "black music" division, but these days no one could define what black music was.

"What in the hell is 'black' music?" she asked her boss one day. "I mean, really, Jim. What is black music?!"

"You know, Tracee, urban music—R&B, rap, hip-hop. Black music."

Tracee didn't want to go down that road with him. What was the purpose? He wouldn't understand. Or perhaps he understood completely, which was an even scarier thought for Tracee. At least if he was ignorant she could feel somewhat okay about working there.

The notion that there needed to be a black music division was one of the most racist things Tracee could imagine. Overwhelmingly more whites bought hip-hop and rap. In fact, about seventy percent of rap music was bought by whites.

"How is that black music?" Tracee thought. "If they depended on blacks to buy rap, there wouldn't be any sales—with all of the bootlegging going on. Blacks will bootleg a CD in a minute. They must be kidding."

What Tracee found out was that having a black music division gave the record companies an excuse to spend less money on promotions, contracts, and other perks than on rock and country. It was a way to keep "those niggas" in their place. While R&B and rap artists like Usher and Nelly outsold both rock and country, both got the tail end of the resources. Hip-hop was influencing an entire culture and an entire generation, but it was getting the short end of the stick in terms of expanding the playing field and developing new artists.

Black music?

It wasn't black music when the Beatles stole their style from Little Richard. It wasn't black music when Tina Turner taught Mick Jagger how to dance and flow. It wasn't black music when Elvis borrowed Chuck Berry's entire act. It was innovative. It was historic. It was music. Janet Jackson, black music. Britney Spears, who does a poor imitation of Janet Jackson, pop star.

Tracee's soul was tired. Soul? She hadn't contemplated that in quite some time. But it was her soul that ached every time it had to witness something crazy, and everything seemed to be getting crazier. Her soul. She needed to find it. And when she did, it needed to be replenished.

She decided for the first time since she was a little girl when her grandmother used to make her say her prayers on the side of the bed every night that she would pray about the situation. It was all uncharted territory but she had nothing to lose. She rediscovered church and joined Harlem's Faith Baptist and started finding some real answers. Tracee even dragged Ritz there one Sunday, and she seemed to enjoy it. That was a breakthrough.

Tracee kept praying and finally an answer came. A decision came down that an executive under her needed to be fired. Tracee wondered why it had to be someone from the black music department. She received a memo stating that her department was overbudget and someone had to go and that they would be well taken care of. She learned that as an executive with more than five years in the company, that person would receive what was called a golden parachute. She decided that that someone should be her. She walked away from her quarter-of-a-million-dollar-a-year job and floated away in her *platinum* parachute that netted her three and a half million, before taxes.

"If I can't live off of that and make it work for me, I'm a damn fool," she said to herself.

Tracee was always good with her money. She was smart enough to buy a loft in the SoHo area in the 1980s when she first got her gig at Uni-Global. The real estate market was down then, and she got an apartment for wonderful price. As she started making more money, she was able to pay it off. Living in the city, she didn't waste money on fancy cars. (She did break down and buy that Lexus right before she left for Florida.) She was well invested in money markets, mutual funds, she had a stock account with Merrill Lynch filled with stocks like Exxon, GE, a concrete stock, and Martha Stewart. (This one turned out to be a real winner. She only bought it because she admired the way Martha did business.) With the platinum parachute, Tracee was set for life.

She picked up and moved to a small town outside of Orlando, Florida, where she had hoped to find some peace and serenity—much needed after the years spent in the music business. She would go back to New York every now and then to check out her friends and get a little dose of the fast lane—Broadway plays, all-night restaurants, and movie premieres.

It was a rare evening when Ritz found herself without any-thing to do. She didn't have any appearances. There were no interviews. No brainstorming sessions with Chas, who had become increasingly busy over the last few months.

Ritz didn't quite know what to do with herself. Her life had changed dramatically. In just a year she had gone from being a fairly successful disc jockey, with a middle- to upper-middle-class lifestyle, to queen of the radio, syndicated around the country, with a very healthy bank account. She had en-dorsements, which included a Denali she didn't drive that much, despite contract stipulations, because Chas said she had an image to keep up and a Denali was a little low-rent and just didn't fit that image.

Ritz bought the car of her dreams and the house of her

dreams—moving from her upscale Jersey City condo to a gated community. She had every material thing she ever imagined. Her mother would be proud. But Ritz hadn't had real fun for more than a year. She hadn't had a real gut-wrenching belly laugh since Tracee moved. And she hadn't had a really good fuck since Kevin. Boy did she miss his strong, confident hands, his talented tongue, and his abnormally thick member. He knew exactly how to use it. But she also missed the safety and security he brought.

Ritz never considered them serious. But he was steady. When she called, he was always there. She never imagined that he would grow tired of the arrangement and want more—something she simply could not give.

"I understand you have a career, but I want a woman—*my* woman—to put me first, Ritz," Kevin said one evening after he'd invited her to go away with him to Bermuda and she'd turned him down. "It's all about your career, Ritz, and all about you. I need more."

Ritz had had nothing to say. He was right. She was on a mission, and at this point in her life she was not going to let anything or anybody—not even a good man and a good lay—get in the way of that.

As she reclined on her six-hundred-thread-count Egyptian sheets, fantasizing about one of the last times she and Kevin were together, Ritz wondered if she had made a mistake.

"No, no, girl, don't go there," she said to herself. "That's just your coochie talking."

It wasn't just talking, it was yelling ghetto-style as Ritz moved her hand over her smooth, chocolaty belly down to her perfectly manicured thatch. She let her middle finger explore between her lips and dip into the hot wetness just below. Ritz let out a light moan. She imagined Kevin sliding in bed behind her, pressing his thick mass lightly into the small of her back and inching down slowly to the opening between her legs. She imagined one of his hands on top of hers, guiding her to all of the secret places that only he seemed to know about. His other hand pinched her nipple lightly. His tongue found the back of her neck and was making its way to her ear. Ritz was writhing in her bed in rapt ecstasy. Kevin had entered her from behind, slipping in just the tip of his member, slowly driving in more and more, faster and faster.

Ritz's hands worked furiously as she was about to explode—
Ring! RIIIIINGGGGGG!
"What the fuck!"
It took Ritz a full minute to realize that the ringing was coming from her phone. It was the guard at the front gate telling her she had a visitor. It took her another thirty seconds to remember that she had called an emergency twenty-four-hour electrician she found in the Yellow Pages. The power in her Jacuzzi was out. Ritz had planned to take a nice long bath this weekend.

She quickly washed her hands in warm vanilla salts, put on her robe and slippers, tried to straighten her hair, and went downstairs to let in the electrician. When she opened the door, she not only let in the electrician, she let in a whole lotta electricity, too. Maybe she was just incredibly horny, or maybe . . .

"Good evening," said the electrician, who introduced himself as Randolph. "Show me where the problem is."

It was too tempting to tell him where the real problem was. So Ritz stood at the door, not saying a word.

"Um, ma'am? It's a little chilly out here. And it costs a lot to heat outside your home."

"Sorry," said Ritz, still a little disoriented. "Come in."

Randolph Jordan had a Morris Chestnut–like smile and deep mocha dimples. He was about six-two and had a line-backer's build. He was neatly dressed in khakis, a Polo turtle-neck, and a Polo jacket with chocolate brown Timberlands. He looked to be in his mid-thirties—it was hard to tell—he was in such great shape, but he could be a little older. After all, forty was the new twenty-five.

Ritz, with her aching loins, had her charm meter up to about a nine and three-quarters out of a possible ten.

"Can I get you something to drink?" Ritz cooed. "Some wine, perhaps?"

"I don't drink, thank you. I'm fine."

You sure are!

"Well, um, how long do you think it will take to fix my hot tub?" Ritz asked. "I just moved in and I don't know what could be wrong with this thing. I've only used it once. I came home today, looking forward to putting on my iPod, lighting some candles, sprinkling in some Aveda salts, and relaxing in the tub. I set the timer to have the water prepared by nine, and nothing happened."

"Don't worry, we'll have you in your bath in no time," he said.

I can only hope!

Ritz sat on the edge of the Jacuzzi as Randolph worked from the access panel on the side of the tub. She leaned over, allowing her robe to open slightly, exposing the fullness of her breasts.

"Can you hand me my wire cutter?" he said, completely ignoring the peep show. "It's next to the screwdriver."

Ritz got the wire cutter, and as she handed it to him she allowed her bare thigh to brush against his hand. She thought she saw him blush.

"Okay, I think it's fixed," he said. "Let's test it out."

He flipped a switch and the bluish LED lights came to life. It was ten-thirty. He set the timer for ten-thirty-one. After one minute the tub was activated. The water, programmed to be exactly 78 degrees, came out of the spout.

"You're in business," he said.

"Excellent!" Ritz said. "Are you sure I can't get you anything?"

"Um, no." Randolph seemed to pause for a bit. "Thank you, again. If you could just sign this work order I'll leave you to your bath."

"Do you have to go?" Ritz said. She hadn't been this bold since . . . Actually, Ritz had never been so bold. She always waited for the man to make the first move. She felt more in control that way, less vulnerable.

"Um . . ." Randolph hesitated again. Ritz thought he might not be prepared.

"I have condoms," said Ritz, remembering that Kevin had left a pack of Magnums in her nightstand drawer. "I hope you can fit Magnums."

She was hoping. If she was going to go out on a limb like this, she wanted that limb to be big, thick, and strong.

Randolph blushed and then broke out into a deep, sexy, nervous laughter.

"I'm sorry," he said. "I just can't believe this."

"Can't believe what?" asked Ritz, getting slightly defensive.

"I can't believe that I am going to go home and take a cold shower," Randolph said. "You are a very beautiful woman and believe me I would love to stay a bit longer, but I can't."

"What?!" Ritz said. "Are you married?"

"No."

"Do you have a girlfriend?" Ritz asked. "Not that it matters, I am not looking for a relationship."

"No."

"Gay?"

"No," he said. "I just want more. I want a meaningful relationship with a woman, and I don't want to spoil it by getting into something frivolous, no matter how tempting it is. And believe me, it's pretty tempting. I made a vow that the next woman I make love to will be my wife."

Ritz paused on that statement. So many emotions ran through her at that moment. She felt cheesy and slightly insulted. It was also a moment of harsh realization.

I'm not marriage material.

"Wow," was all Ritz could muster. "I respect that. I'm sorry. I'm really not like that at all."

"You have no reason to apologize," Randolph said. "Believe me, you did nothing wrong. If you'd caught me six months ago . . . well, let's just says things would be different. Very different."

"There I go with my fucked-up timing!" Ritz laughed. "So what happened six months ago? Or who happened?"

"Who? That's an interesting question," said Randolph. "It's a long story. A lot of it has to do with my father and watching him and how he's been with women—never really committing himself to anything or anyone. I guess I saw myself following in his footsteps and I didn't like it."

"At least you know who your father is," said Ritz. "I have never met my father. And I'm kind of glad. I don't have any images of an imperfect man who may have mistreated my mother, screwing me up with a whole bunch of problems—as if I don't have enough. But that's another story for another day."

"I'd like to hear it," Randolph said with a soft smile spreading across his face. "You're a very interesting woman, Ritz Harper."

"Maybe we can pretend the proposition never happened,"

Ritz chuckled. "And maybe we can start over. You never know, I could be that woman you're looking for."

"You never know," Randolph said. "Now sign this paper so I can get out of here before you make me forget my promise to myself."

"I'm still hoping," said Ritz with a wink. Randolph crossed his arms across his broad chest and gave her a look.

"Okay, okay. Where do I sign? Geez, you can't blame a sister for trying, can you?"

"Okay, good-night, Ms. Harper," he said, heading for the door. "It was a pleasure meeting you. If you have any other *electrical* problems, call me."

Ritz grabbed his hand as he reached to open the door.

"Hey, thank you for being a good man," Ritz said. "I haven't encountered one of those in a while. Please forgive my naughty behavior. Perhaps I can call you sometime when I don't have an electrical problem."

Randolph put his hand over hers, cupping it between his big, but surprisingly soft, hands.

"You can call me anytime," he said.

18

ON THE AIR

"Okay, I believe that people have lost their damn minds," Ritz said. "Two crazy stories I was reading on my way in today. One is about a woman who had broken up with her husband but let him move back in. I didn't need to read the rest to figure out that it wasn't going to work out. I mean, when does 'reconciliation' actually work? There's usually so much baggage and nasty feelings that all it takes is one thing to send that relationship right back into hell. Well, that's what happened here. But this woman took it to another level. Apparently she and her husband got into a fight. So what does she do? She starts throwing his stuff out of the window. But she can't stop at his clothes. She has to pick up his eight-month-old, three-pound Yorkie and toss him out of the window, too. That little doggie didn't have a chance. Splat! Oh, did I mention, they lived on the tenth floor of a high-rise complex. She told the cops she didn't mean to throw out the dog, she thought it was a fuzzy shirt."

"Daaaaaaayum!" yelped Aaron, as he hit the sound effect of a howling dog. "That's just cold-blooded!"

"Well, if you think that's cold-blooded, listen to this next story. A West New York woman was arrested for throwing her newborn son out of a third-story window and into the air-shaft of her apartment building. The baby, thank God, landed on a pile of garbage and survived. His tiny skull is fractured though.

"This story makes me so mad that I feel like hunting that bitch down and hanging her from her feet off of the Empire State Building and dropping her on her head. How helpless was this little baby. He didn't ask his skanky mama to spread her young legs and let some man screw her. He didn't ask to come here and have her dumb ass not be able to take care of him and then have the nerve to try to kill him. Do you know how many people want a child and can't have one? The dumb ass could have given him to a loving home!"

Ritz began to tear up. It was one of her few soft spots.

"That little baby just needed someone to love him," Ritz said, sniffling. "I can't believe how cruel people can be. And get this! There's more to this story. This isn't the first time this crack ho has done something like this. And yes, I am calling her a crack ho because that's the only kind of animal that could do something like this. They found a mummified corpse of another full-term baby underneath a pack of cigarettes in the same apartment. They believe this, too, was a baby of this crazed crack ho."

The phone lines began to light up.

"You're on with Ritz!"

"This is Paula from Harlem. Ritz, I'll help you hunt down that animal! Me and my husband have been trying to have a baby for years. I can't afford fertility treatments and this bitch wants to just throw babies away?!"

"I know," Ritz said. "I am so angry, I can barely keep my composure. Thank you for your call and I'll let you know when hunting season is in. Next caller."

"You need to shut your fucking mouth, bitch!" The caller had a brutal bite to her voice. Aaron bleeped the "fucking" but kept the bitch—it made good radio.

"Who is this?"

"You will know exactly who this if you keep running your mouth! You need to get your facts straight. That's the problem I have about you—always talking and running your mouth without your shit being right."

"I'm reading directly from the *New York Times*. You can't get more accurate than that!"

"Well, you need to read the *whole* story, dumb bitch! That woman you are talking about is my sister. She's not a crack ho or a dumb ass or anything else you have been saying about her. She is a victim. Her father—our father—has been raping her since she was seven. He had been raping me, too. I was lucky. I never got pregnant. She did. There was no way she could love that child or take care of that child, knowing who his father is, knowing what he did to her. How could she? Could you?!"

Ritz was speechless. She could only manage an "Um."

"Hell, no! You probably would have killed yourself. But my sister kept moving. She was an A student. She planned to go to college and move out on her own, as I was able to do. But you know everything! You just sit on your perch and condemn people as if you're perfect. You have no clue! You need to do your homework. Better yet, you need to shut the fuck up. You want to kick people when they're down? Like my sister doesn't have enough to deal with. I'm going to show you how that feels, bitch!"

The caller hung up. There was silence in the studio. All eyes were on Ritz, wondering what her next move would be.

"Just like a coward to hang up the phone. I don't care what you're going through, that first baby didn't deserve to die and that second precious baby doesn't deserve to be in a hospital with a cracked skull. And while I am sympathetic to the horrors of incest, the reality is that we all have things we have to go through in life. That's life. No one is exempt. But you don't compound your situation by inflicting harm on others."

The words hung in the air, and for the first time they rang true to Ritz. Her own words stung her. She shook it off, though, because she had a show to do.

It's a cliché, but reality: The show must always go on.

19

Edwin Lakes stood in the pulpit of Faith Baptist and marveled at how every single seat was filled, even the balcony. They had to have a room with monitors for the overflow. They had just built this church, and it seemed that they already needed to expand again.

There were few areas where the Edwin disagreed with his father, who had started Faith Baptist. Their only verbal disagreement happened to be over the direction of the ministry. Senior Pastor Lakes wanted to keep the church small and intimate. He felt that to truly teach the word, he needed a congregation of only those who truly wanted to learn the word. He believed in sifting his flock like wheat.

"The Bible says that narrow is the way, son. And only a few will make it into heaven."

"Yeah, Dad. But how do you know if it will be *your* few?"

Edwin would argue. "Jesus calls us to cast our net wide. I think we have a better chance reaching those few by expanding our horizons. If we attract more people, we can save more souls."

"Son, you have to be careful about mixing your messages," Senior Pastor Lakes would say. "You can't serve two masters. And what you're talking about is very close to that."

"Dad, Jesus started with only twelve disciples and now look how huge His church is," Edwin said. "Jesus had a vision. I have a vision."

"Be careful, son," his father said. "Be careful. I'll pray about it, and I want you to pray about it, too."

Both Edwins prayed a lot. Even when younger Edwin questioned whether he would indeed take over the ministry his father started, he never questioned his love for God or his desire to help people know God. Edwin Jr. had few regrets on his journey. Very few.

Once he took over Faith Baptist, it didn't take long for Edwin to begin to realize his vision. His style was a departure from his father's old-time religion. Edwin was young, he was very handsome, and he was charismatic. His command of the word was unrivaled. He was well trained. He was his father's son—he had a great understanding of the Bible and how to teach it. But he also appealed to the younger generation, which had long turned their back on the traditional black church. They were coming out to Faith Baptist, though.

By Edwin's second year, the church had grown as much in stature as in size. It was not unusual to see Star Jones

Reynolds and her husband, Al, seated in the front row. Even Pastor Mason Betha aka MA$E, who had returned to rap after starting his own ministry in Atlanta, would spend Sunday there when he was in town.

Sunday by Sunday, Edwin seemed to get stronger and better. He learned that running a church the size of Faith Baptist was more like running a corporation, and his undergraduate degree in business came in handy.

During those two years of building the church, Edwin met and married Patricia Longly—a Spelman graduate who was working as a schoolteacher. She got pregnant quickly and they had a son, Edwin III. About seventeen months later, they had another on the way. That was nearly two years ago. The *Ebony* cover piece had been planned way in advance. By the time the piece came out, little Ashley was almost walking.

Edwin rarely thought about the times before he took over the church from his father. He rarely, if ever, thought about Miami. It was his past. He now had a present and a future that he loved and that needed his undivided attention. He had a wife, two small children, and a nearly eight-thousand-member church in a building that only held three thousand. He was preaching three services on Sunday to accommodate everyone. They were about three years away from building a new church. Edwin was pleased with the progress and pleased with his life.

He never looked back.

His mother, Minnie Lakes, was also happy—as happy as

she could be without her doting husband. She was proud of what her son had been able to accomplish in such a short time. Edwin never thought his mother would be happy again. His father's death had been a horrible blow to her because they both shared the same dream. They wanted to spread the word of God and make the church a foundation, a true source of strength for the surrounding community. Minnie and Edwin Sr. were as close as any couple Edwin had known. They were the Ossie Davis and Ruby Dee of the church crowd. They shared everything, and together they built Faith Baptist.

Mother Lakes completely doted and depended on Edwin. He was her rock.

"Without you, baby, this church would have fallen apart," she told him on more than one occasion.

Little did she know that *with* him, the end result might be the same.

20

"Ritz, girl! Are you ready for this! This might be your best show yet!" Chas came strutting into the studio like a peacock.

"Do tell!!!!!" Ritz said. She was always thirsty and Chas always had the water. Ritz and Chas had a symbiotic relationship. She was well aware the she couldn't do the show without him. When she wanted to take it to the next level and had no idea how, Chas provided a way and they moved forward. Ritz was a radio pro, she had great delivery, but Chas kept the drama flowing. That was the reason why her ratings kept climbing: The stakes kept getting raised.

Chas kept strolling around the studio and refused to tell her the news.

"Okay, Mr. Thing, you got two more minutes on that runway and you better give up the goods!" Ritz said as she grabbed his arm and playfully pinched it.

"Ouch!" Chas howled. "Girl, you know I bruise easy! Okay, okay!"

"That's better," Ritz said.

"So you know that man I left Club Red with last Friday night?"

"Who could miss him?" Ritz said. "I didn't want to say anything because I know how you are about your business. But who could miss two of God's gifts to women strolling out the door with each other! I think I saw at least a dozen sisters rolling their eyes when you two left, practically arm in arm."

"Yes, girl, I can't blame them," Chas said. "We were fine, weren't we! Anyway, honey. Wait till you hear this!"

"Okay, I've waited long enough. Spill it!"

"Ritz, you remember that preacher that they featured on the cover of this month's *Ebony*?"

"Yeah?"

"The one with the beautiful wife and the one-point-two children and the doting mother."

"Yeah?"

"The one with the really, really big church in Harlem with all of those people like Puffy and Star Jones Reynolds or whatever she's calling herself in attendance."

"Will you spit it out already! What about him!!!!"

"Well!" Chas said. "That Mr. Preacher Man was once in a relationship."

"With . . . ?"

"The man I left the club with on Friday," Chas said. "His name is Ivan."

Over the past few years Ritz had heard everything—from the callers to the real-life celebrity gossip items. But this little diddy left her almost speechless.

"Shut *up!*"

That was all she could muster. Ritz had been to Pastor Edwin Lakes's church with Tracee before she moved south. Ritz had had a strained relationship with God since He took her mother, but she still believed in Him. She did, however, hate the whole organized church thing. She thought it was too much. But this preacher seemed to be one of the few who she could relate to. He delivered the message with utmost clarity, the way her favorite teacher had taught her Shakespeare—which she loved to this day.

Pastor Lakes was so real without trying to appeal to the "ghetto," as so many ministers tried to do. He delivered his message without appearing to be above his congregation. He was a true teacher of the word, and Ritz found it refreshing. Chas had never given her a single item that turned out to be false. Not one. But she was hoping that this would be the first.

"But wait, child, there's more," Chas said.

Ritz was thinking "Please, no more!"

"Ivan is coming to the studio today to put the pastor on blast," Chas said. "I got him to agree to give you an exclusive."

"Damn! You must have really put it on him!" said Ritz.

"Yes I did!" Chas said, giving her a high-five. "I guess he wants a little revenge. It seems that our good pastor left my boy high and very dry without as much as a good-bye—not even a Dear John letter. Nothing."

"Damn!" Ritz said. "Wow. Today? What time can we expect this atomic bomb to be dropped? We have to alert the media."

"I am already ahead of you," Chas said. " 'Page Six,' *Entertainment Tonight*, 'Rush & Molloy.' Everyone has been put on high alert to tune in today at five."

Ritz's mixed emotions got clear real quick. She started getting excited, as she always did when she knew she was about to make news again. She loved this part of her job and she loved Chas for always delivering the goods. She had to take a few minutes to prepare her questions. Ritz never wrote any questions down, but she had to organize in her mind the most dramatic way for the story to unfold. Her flair for the dramatic was one of her best gifts. And she had been honing that one for a while—in radio there was no one better at giving drama.

After all, drama was her middle name!

21

It was an official day out for the girls. Patricia Lakes had marked it on her calendar the week before after she finished choir rehearsal, and she was looking forward to it. While most of the women at the church were reluctant to speak with Patricia and were even standoffish, Kimberly Atkins embraced her. She didn't care about Patricia being the church's first lady. Patricia was a lady first and from what Kim could see, she needed a good girlfriend to hang out with. Kim elected herself to be the one.

Kim treated Patricia like a regular person because she *was* a regular person. And Patricia appreciated it. She hated being put up on a pedestal. She hated the distance her position gave her from everyone else. But Kim was a bridge.

While Kim was definitely a true Christian, she didn't take

any mess and she let people know what was what. "Jesus didn't bite His tongue," she would say. "And neither will I."

Most people were afraid of Kim because while she was gregarious she also had a tongue that could only be described as a welder's flame—it burned. But it burned with the purpose of bringing things to together. At a church the size of Faith Baptist, Kim had a whole lot of work to do.

If choir practice was running long and everyone was getting frustrated, it would be Kim to speak up. "Um, Choir Director Jones, it's time to go!" She didn't do it in a disrespectful manner. She actually used humor—the kind of humor where people weren't sure if she was being funny or not. Patricia loved her bluntness and brutal honesty—even though sometimes it was a little too much for even Patricia.

Patricia admired Kim. She admired her spunk because it was very effective.

Kim was there when Edwin's father was the pastor. And she was there when Edwin took over. She witnessed all of the fasting and praying that went on among a lot of the women in the congregation who were praying to God that Edwin would choose them to be their wife.

Kim was also there when Edwin sifted the wheat from the chaff and found Patricia. She witnessed the shock and envy when the pastor introduced Patricia as his fiancée.

And when some started whispering "She's an outsider. She's not even a member. How could he?"

Kim would shoot back, "I didn't know that there could be

any *outsiders* within the body of Christ. I wonder what Jesus would think about that?" And the chatter quickly ceased.

Kim had Patricia's back before Patricia even knew that there was a Kim. So it was natural that they would become friends. They had a lot in common—handsome, God-fearing husbands. Both had young children and felt that they had no time for themselves. After their last choir rehearsal, Kim decided in Kim fashion to make a stand. She decided that she had enough of the ripping and running and doing for everyone else.

"Patty, girl, we are going to a spa!" Kim announced.

"A what?!" Patricia said.

"A spa," she said. "You know, facials, massages, green tea, that music that sounds like running water, the whole nine. I am getting a babysitter for the kids and we are going for the entire day to be pampered."

"But—"

"But nothing!" Kim said. "I'll not hear anything from you but 'What time do we leave'!"

Kim called Patricia the day before their spa date to make sure she hadn't chickened out. Patricia was getting little Edwin ready for preschool.

"Girl, I just wanted to confirm that we are on," Kim said. "Not that you have a choice or anything!"

Patricia grinned. "Yes, we're on. Okay!"

Patricia was thinking how she might slowly be able to build a social life for herself again that included life outside of the church and her home. She hadn't had any real girlfriends since college, and somehow she had drifted away from all of them. She had no one but herself to blame because she loved her family so much. But she was starting to feel empty and needed to balance her life. Edwin was a great husband and a good friend, but he had so much weight on him with the church and he was constantly busy.

"Don't forget, you have to be here by ten-thirty," Kim said. "Our treatments begin at eleven. I figured after the spa we could go shopping and then have a nice meal."

"I can't wait!"

Dieci in Linnoston, New Jersey, was one of the best full-service spas in the tristate area. It even had a sauna, a gym, and a swimming pool for those who wanted to exercise. Kim and Patricia didn't want to do any work. They wanted to be served during their experience, and they got the works.

It was the most relaxation Patricia had experienced since her honeymoon in Bermuda. She missed the pampering. She even got a pedicure—something she hadn't bothered to do in years.

"Edwin's going to love that shade of pink," Kim said.

Patricia smiled just thinking about it. She loved the attention Edwin gave her, and she wanted to make him happy. This would be a nice treat for him, too.

After the spa they headed across the highway to The Mall at Short Hills. Patricia only went shopping for kids' clothes and kids' accessories and shirts and ties for Edwin. She loved shopping for them.

"Girl, you desperately need a pair of jeans," Kim said. "Just because you're a pastor's wife doesn't mean you need to look like it all of the time!"

They shared a chuckle and headed to the Gap. Kim had just turned thirty. Patricia, who was thirty-two, was dressing like she was much older.

"A pair of Gap jeans will give you some of your sass back," Kim said. "But let's stay out of the low-rider section, okay? I don't think Edwin would appreciate that! And neither would God!"

After shopping, the two headed over to Café Arugula's, an upscale Italian restaurant on South Orange Avenue in South Orange. On the drive there, Kim turned on the radio. She normally played a gospel CD, a compilation featuring her favorite, Vanessa Bell Armstrong. But the radio came on. It was preset to 99.9, WHOT.

Every now and then Kim liked to listen to Ritz Harper, even though she would usually have to pray about it later and repent.

"Okay, everybody, we have in the studio with us today Ivan Richardson," Ritz cooed. "He's a very handsome man about six foot even. Chocolately skin that is as smooth . . . Ooh, let me feel that . . . yep, as smooth as a baby's ass. What kind of products do you use?"

"Kiehls," Ivan said.

"Okay. Welcome, Ivan, to the show," Ritz said. "Okay, so . . . do you consider yourself a gay man? Or are you like J. L. King, 'on the down low'? Whatever that means."

"I hate labels," Ivan said. "I don't label myself. I just prefer an attractive man's company. And it's not all physical for me; there has to be something more."

"Uh-huh," Ritz said, nodding in agreement. "So, Ivan, I understand that a while back you had something more and that something more left you in a lurch—without so much as a good-bye."

"Well, Ritz, it's deeper than that. I met him by chance and it was love at first sight, at least it was for me. He was so gentle and kind. I had never met a person like him. He had a strength about him, a power that was intoxicating. He told me that I was his first—his very first.

"It was whirlwind. We shared a lot over the period of time we spent together, and during that time we spent every waking moment together. Ritz, it was the best time I have ever had in my life. I thought that even if we didn't continue our relationship, we would be friends for life. I mean, he shared things with me that I know he never shared with anyone else."

"So what happened?" Ritz said, leaning forward as if to grab the words right from his mouth. Then she shot a look at Aaron to let him know to get ready with the appropriate sound effects. She always had her show working like a well-directed Broadway play.

"That's a good question. I'm still trying to figure that out. I'd gone out for a meeting with some clients for most of the afternoon. We had plans that evening to check out a new restaurant that had just opened downtown. We were going to celebrate our eighth-month anniversary—yes, I know it was corny, but we were getting down like that. I had even bought us a two-seater scooter to tool around on as a surprise for our anniversary. We had rented one that we'd had a blast on.

"I got home around four in the afternoon and the place was empty. His clothes were gone, all of his toiletries, all traces of him. Gone. Not a note, nothing. And what was so hurtful, Ritz, was that I had no way of tracking him down. It was strange. You can share so much with someone, get so deep with them, fall so hard, and not really know much about them. I knew he was from New York, but I never thought about getting a number for him there. Why would I? I never imagined he would just pick up and leave."

"So why not call information?" Ritz said. "Why not go on the Internet and track him down? You had a name, right?"

"Yes, I had a name," Ivan said, getting a little choked up just thinking about it. It was an old wound that was cracking open, feeling like it all just happened yesterday even though it had been nearly seven years. "I am a proud man, Ritz. My mama and grandmama raised me to bow to no man, to not show weakness. I wasn't running after anyone like some lovesick puppy. He disrespected me and he ripped my heart from my chest. I was not giving him the satisfaction of having me stalk him. That just isn't me."

"But you had a name," Ritz said. "You could have called just to tell him off and let him know how you felt."

"I was not going to give him the satisfaction. Besides, there was a part of me that absolutely loved him and didn't want to disrupt his world. I mean, he *is* a minister."

Kim and Patricia were talking while the radio was on. But when the man spoke the word "minister," they both perked up.

"A minister?!" Ritz pretended to act surprised.

"Yes."

Kim couldn't believe it. "I am so tired of these false prophets infiltrating our churches," she exclaimed. "Folks are showing up to church and they have no idea who's really standing in their pulpit. 'Devil's henchmen' is what I call them."

"Girl!" was all Patricia could muster.

Ritz Harper was reeling Ivan in for the final round.

"Is this minister someone we would all know?" Ritz said, baiting Ivan.

"Yes. Now, I'm not here to out him. But I feel that people should know the kind of man who is leading a tremendous amount of people. I believe he is a good man, but he is a liar. He's lying to his family and I believe that he is lying to himself. And what is it that they say, Ritz? The truth will . . . what?"

"Set you free!" Ritz said, finishing the statement. "So who is this mystery minister?

"What prompted me to come here today was seeing how happy he looked. But underneath the smile I saw on his face, I know that he was happier with me. I want to rescue him from this lie of a life that he's leading. I want him to come face-to-face with what I know, and that is that he's really a gay man. I want Pastor Edwin Lakes to be set free."

Kim almost ran off the road. She immediately looked at

Patricia, who looked like she had been hit in the face with a ten-pound bag of flour. The color had completely drained from her face and she looked beaten.

"Wha-at?" Patricia screeched.

Ritz let the silence linger, milking the moment for all she could. The studio was wild with shocked awe and gasps. Then Aaron hit a button and played the "I'm gay, I'm a homo, I like guys!" sound effect.

"Pastor Edwin Lakes," Ritz repeated the name. "That's the minister who recently was featured on the cover of *Ebony*. He has one of the largest churches in Harlem. *That* Pastor Edwin Lakes?"

"Yes, that Pastor Edwin Lakes!"

Patricia was instantly nauseous.

"Kim, take me home, please," Patricia said in almost a whisper.

"Of course" was all Kim said for the rest of the ride. It was one of the few times in her entire life that Kimberly Atkins was at a loss for words.

22

Ivan left the studio and walked down Park Avenue in hopes of catching a cab back to his hotel. But before he realized it, he had walked fifteen blocks and decided to just keep walking. He had to clear his head, which was full of so much conflict and confusion.

He thought he would feel better releasing seven years of bitterness and anger. He thought he would feel free letting Edwin have it for making him feel so cheap and so small. Revenge wasn't sweet for Ivan; it churned in his stomach like broken glass.

"What am I doing?" he thought to himself. It was a question he wished he had asked *before* he'd gone on the radio and completely ruined Edwin's life. "What have I done?"

That answer was clear. Ivan did something he thought he wasn't capable of doing—he had acted out of cowardice. Instead of being a man and facing Edwin, asking him what happened or, even better, moving on with his life, Ivan took the coward's way out: He broadsided him.

"I knew how to reach him," Ivan started muttering to himself. "I could have just called him. I'm sure he had a good reason for what he did.

"Yeah, but he should have called me or written me. He didn't have to leave me out there hanging like that. Who did he think he was?"

This battle went back and forth inside of Ivan's head as he aimlessly walked the streets of New York.

23

Derek hated the long ride upstate. But he made the trip religiously once a month. He didn't have to ride the bus, but he wanted to feel some of the pain his brother must be feeling, locked away like an animal. He felt grimy being on that yellow school bus, riding through those backwoods with all of the depressed family members—mostly mothers, a few girlfriends, a wife or two, and a handful of kids—of men who were locked away, some (like his brother) who would be there for a very long time.

Derek was practically the only male besides the bus driver on the trip. He was also one of the few who seemed to have a little money in his pockets. It was all very disheartening. But it was a necessary evil. Derek was a man of his word. When his brother got locked up—sentenced to fifteen years to life on a racketeering conviction—he vowed that he would take care of him. Derek kept Jayrod's commissary account well stocked and gladly received the collect calls Jayrod made every week.

Family loyalty was something instilled in the Mentor brothers from an early age by their mother. She wasn't much of a mother to them in many ways, but she beat one thought into them that stuck: "Family is all you got, you two are all you got. So when the world crumbles in on you, hold on to each other."

Their mother had died ten years ago, when Jayrod was twenty and Derek was seventeen. She was found in a crack den with a needle in her arm, overdosed on heroin. Jayrod became the father and mother, provider and caretaker—a role he had been playing long before their mother actually died. Jay hit the streets hard and made sure that neither he nor Derek wanted for anything. He kept Derek out of trouble because "You are the good one," he told his brother. "You are going to college, and you're going to be a lawyer. I'm damn sure going to need a good one sooner or later."

Unfortunately, sooner came a lot sooner than any of them expected. Before Derek could make it out of college, Jayrod was locked up.

It was Ritz Harper who put the heat on Jayrod. She was constantly talking about how the rap game had been infiltrated by the drug game and how so many of these rap labels were headed by drug lords and king pins. Killer Inc., which featured platinum-selling Da Ruler and R&B sensation Empathy, was started by an associate of Jayrod's who ran one of the largest drug rings in the Bronx. After Gato went "legit" in music, he used Jayrod as a supplier. Ritz Harper was fascinated by the connections. When artists came by the studio, she got them to admit that they had a steady person supplying them with their weed. Under the guise of trying to find a supplier for herself whom she could trust, she got some artists to give up a name. Once Ritz had a name, she ran with it.

"It must nice to be the elite supplier to the stars," Ritz said on the air. "That Jayrod Mentor must have a nice business for himself. Because one of his boys, Mr. Bones, couldn't even sit through a twenty-minute interview in this studio without lighting up twice . . . cough, cough!"

The feds tuned in to the *Ritz Harper Excursion* for information as well as entertainment. And they started watching Jayrod. He started feeling the heat and had to be extremely careful. But you can't be careful enough when the feds are on your trail. And thanks to the Patriot Act, where there were no limits on what the government can spy on, they would get you for something.

Like Al Capone and Tommy Mickens and so many others before him—Jayrod Mentor didn't get caught for the obvious. He was caught for tax evasion and racketeering.

At the prison, Derek stood in line and waited his turn to go through the solid metal doors where he had to endure a search by a stoic, stone-faced guard. Derek then had to empty the contents of his pockets, which were placed in a large manila envelope and locked in a locker. He was told he would get his belongings back upon leaving the prison. Derek felt a little more humiliated, and he didn't like it. He knew his strong-willed brother was going crazy. Jayrod's only saving grace was that he had lots of friends inside. In jail, he was a bit of a celebrity and was well taken care of for someone who was stripped of everything, including the ability to decide when to wake up and when to go to sleep.

Derek was led into a room divided in two by a piece of Plexiglas that reached the ceiling. Jayrod sat on one side in a prison-issue orange jumpsuit. Derek sat in the hardback chair on the other side and picked up the phone.

"Yo, thanks for that last deposit," Jayrod said. "It came in handy. How's the business?"

"It's going well," Derek said.

"You staying out of sight, because you know they would love nothing better than to have you in this place, too."

"I know. I'm being very careful."

"I know you are. You were raised right," Jayrod said with a wink. "Listen, I talked to my lawyer and they are filing an appeal. It's going to cost us a mint. Can you cover it?"

"Sure."

"That's my baby brother! Okay. Good. I'm going crazy in here, D. I know I can't do no fifteen years in this place. That bitch Ritz Harper has to pay. This is her fault. The big-mouth bitch. I have everything set up, D. It's all in place. I just need you to oversee it and make the payoffs. Can I count on you?"

"You don't even have to ask," Derek said. "Of course you can count on me."

"I couldn't believe our good luck. I mean, what are the

odds of you banging the intern who works right under that bitch. How lucky could we get? You now have access to her every move. This is perfect. So again, my boys are ready. Everything is in place. All you have to do is make the call and give them the place and then make sure they get hit off when the deed is done. If this appeal doesn't go through, at least I can be in here with a smile on my face. I love you, baby brother."

"I love you, too, Jay."

Derek hung up the phone, collected his stuff, and rode the bus back to Penn Station. Drugs were one thing. But murder? And what about Jamie? Derek had feelings for her. But he also had a strange attraction to Ritz. He would have to end it with Jamie. He would have to do it today.

24

It was less than twenty-four hours since Ritz Harper and Ivan Richardson had tossed away a lifetime of dreams, a lifetime of service. In one hour, everything that Edwin's parents had hoped for, for him and their church, was fading away. He was on the verge of losing everything—his wife, his church, perhaps even his faith.

Friday mornings at First Baptist Church were some of the best times for Edwin. He loved seeing the grand church empty. He got to appreciate the light as it reflected through the stained glass onto the beige stone floor. The carpeted pulpit, with its rich cherrywood, looked like a regal throne. Being here all alone allowed him to take in the wonderment and enormity of the mission he believed he was on. Edwin was impressed and thankful and in awe that God had allowed every seat in this cavernous building to be filled every Sunday. This Friday, though, was not so rosy.

Edwin walked down the middle aisle of the church and turned right before the pulpit. He opened a large wooden door that led to a long hallway filled with rooms on either side. Two of the rooms were computer rooms. The other rooms were for different classes being held at the church for adults and children after school.

When he arrived at the church's library, he put his hand on the knob but, before going in, he asked God to give him the strength to deal with whatever was waiting for him on the other side.

"Good morning everyone," Edwin said. The room was filled with members of the church council—the inner circle, comprised of select deacons and deaconesses, trustees and elders. Some were making the meeting before heading to work, some were retired, some had taken the day off. Most were seated at the large tables in the middle of the room. There was no need for Edwin to guess what they were talking about. They were so into their conversations about him that most hadn't realized that the very reason they were at the church on a Friday morning had just arrived.

Deacon Samson Lee cleared his throat to let everyone know that the meeting was about to start. Edwin walked toward the front of the room and the door opened again. It was the final arrival—Edwin's mother, Mother Lakes. (Patricia, his wife, was not there. She told him she needed space.)

Edwin's mother commanded respect not just from her congregation but also from the community. She had dedicated her life to helping others. The church for her wasn't some detached thing that she happened to be a part of. That church was part of her spirit; it was in her blood.

"Good morning, Mother Lakes!" everyone seemed to say in unison.

Edwin couldn't help but think how they sounded so much like rehearsed children. He was certain his mother had timed her arrival so she wouldn't be forced to sit in a room where people were passing judgment on her son. She took a seat behind the long wooden desk at the front of the room. A half podium had been brought in and placed in the center of the table.

Deacon Lee, Edwin's father's best friend, had remained loyal to the family and was a godsend after Pastor Lakes Sr. died. He took care of a lot of the transitional details for Edwin, making his ascension to pastor so much smoother. Deacon Lee knew all of the ins and outs of running the church. He was the eyes and ears of the church. He was a strong man, a man who took charge. Even Edwin's mother grew to depend on him. Deacon Lee cleared his throat again, bringing the room of fifty-five-plus to attention.

"We are here this morning, as you know, because horrible accusations have been brought against our pastor and our leader, Edwin Lakes."

Shouts of amen came from all over the room.

"Pastor Lakes, first I would like to say that I am behind you one hundred percent," Deacon Lee continued. "Those liars and evildoers who have tainted your name will feel the wrath of the Almighty!

"I would also like to say, and I speak on behalf of everyone here, that this is just a formality. We as elders of the church simply want to witness with our own eyes and hear with our own ears you denounce these lies with your own mouth."

Deacon Lee turned to Edwin and Mother Lakes and gestured to show he was finished speaking. He turned the floor over to Edwin.

Edwin gently let go of his mother's hand and placed it back on her own lap. Then he cleared his throat and stood to his feet.

"Deacon Lee, I would like to thank you for your support," Edwin started. "I would also like to thank each and every one of you who are present today. You are truly the backbone of this church.

"I stand before you today not as a guilty man."

Amens erupted in the room. Sister Sarah Parker, head of the usher board, could be heard saying, "I knew it! The devil sure is busy, though!"

"Please, please," Edwin said. "Let me finish."

"Ain't no need to finish," said Rosco Banks, the seventy-six-year-old church organist. He took the hat he had resting on his lap and put it on his head and started to gather his coat, too. "That's all I needed to hear!"

"I would like to finish," Edwin cut in. "Everyone, please settle down."

"You all quiet down!" said Evelene Washington. "The reverend is not done. You all show some respect." Sister Washington was used to bringing order to a room. She had been the head Sunday school teacher since Faith Baptist moved to its large facility. She presided over three teachers and more than a hundred fifty students every Sunday morning.

"I stand before you as a man of God, a man who has been honored to be a part of this church and who has served this church and its members to the best of my ability," Edwin continued. "I cannot say that I'm without sin or without a past. But I can say that today and all the days since I was made head of this church that I have been a righteous man, a righteous leader. Not a single person in this room is without sin. But I can say that every true follower of Christ that sits before me has been forgiven and washed clean in the eyes of God.

"If anyone in this room has a problem with what I have said and no longer wants to be part this church that I believe was built on a foundation of love, then please take up your mat and walk.

"If there is nothing else, I'll address this entire situation in a sermon on Sunday morning, and I encourage any member to see me or write me if they have any further questions. I trust that you elders will do the same and reach out to me if you have any further questions or concerns. Thank you all for coming here today. I appreciate and love each and every one of you."

As Edwin stood before the group, there was a silence that

seemed to last for hours. Finally Edwin's mother broke the stillness and walked up and hugged her son and smiled.

Deacon Lee came up and shook Edwin's hand firmly. He turned to Mother Lakes and said, "If you need anything, Minnie, please call. You know I am behind you."

Everyone began to file out of the room, speaking in hushed tones. Edwin didn't think one person would have the guts to confront him on the matter. He knew they would rather discuss half-truths and spread them throughout the congregation.

"I'm going by the house to help Patricia out with the kids," Edwin's mother said to him. "I know she's not taking this very well."

"I know, Ma," Edwin said. "Thank you for everything. I have a lot of e-mails that I need to answer and then I'll be on my way home."

By this time, the library was empty except for Edwin and his mother.

"Ma, I'm so sorry!" Edwin said. "I didn't mean to ruin everything. I don't want to destroy your life's work. When I get home, we can discuss finding a pastor to replace me. After my sermon on Sunday, I am resigning."

His mother wrapped her arms around him and pulled him close to her ample bosom. "Baby, it's not up to you. This is God's work, this is God's church, and no one can ruin that," she said. "We will pray about this as we do about everything, and it will be all right. Just be still, baby. Just be still.

"My faith is not an act. It is a way of life," his mother continued. "And it's not just for me but for you, too, Edwin. God will see us through this—as He has seen us through everything else. We will stay together and will let God fight this battle. Who are these people to judge and not forgive? Each member of this church must look into their spirits and figure out why they come to church and why they read the word.

"Your leaving will not save the church. This is not a physical battle, it is a spiritual one. And just because you leave doesn't mean that battle is over."

Edwin, whose eyes had begun to well up, grabbed tight to his mother as he tried to regulate his breathing.

"Edwin, it's going to be okay," she said as her voice began to crack. Edwin was trying to be strong as he always had. But Edwin could no longer keep up the front. He hated himself for all the pain and embarrassment he was causing his family. He could no longer hold the fire burning the edges of his eyes back as he and his mother stood in the middle of the church library weeping in each other's arms.

25

The newspapers and all of the cable outlets, from BET to *Entertainment Tonight*, picked up the Pastor Lakes exposé. Of course, Ritz was getting all of the credit. Ritz had almost certainly ruined the career of a very beloved minister—taking him down with one salacious interview. And while she wasn't gloating too much, she was happy about the press she was getting. It was so surreal that she floated through her shift not even noticing that it was time to leave. She was so caught up in her own smell that she totally ignored Chas. She didn't even thank him.

But for Ritz, everything was going according to plan. She was on her way to clearing more stations and then television. She would be queen of all media, just as she had envisioned.

Ritz was in her pink office, going over the latest graft from a star. It was a package that included jeans and the latest J.Lo fragrance from Jennifer Lopez's Sweetface Company.

Chas didn't believe in sulking. He was the master of the masks. So he put on his happy face and kept it moving.

"You did your thing, girlie!" he said, trying to prompt some gratitude.

"Yes, I did," she said. "I mean, *we* did! Team, group hug!"

Ritz gathered Chas and Aaron and Jamie over into a huddle.

"I love you guys!" she said. "I couldn't do this without you. Thank you."

"Baby, it's all you," Chas said.

"Ritz, you're the best," Jamie said.

"Oh, what an ass kisser," Aaron said to Jamie. "Wipe that shit off your lips!"

"Aaron, shut up," Ritz said. "My ass is far too clean for me to leave any stains."

They all broke into laughter.

"Oh, and, Jamie, I almost forgot . . ."

"Yes?" Jamie said.

"Can you come in a little early on Monday before the show?" Ritz said. "There's something I need to talk to you about."

"Uh-oh," Aaron said.

"Sure, Ritz," said Jamie, a little nervous. Ritz could be filled with drama and suspense, but now she actually sounded excited. She was going to offer Jamie a full-time position as an assistant producer. In addition to getting Ritz's hair for her weaves and buying her weekly and monthly magazines and daily papers, she would be given some booking responsibilities and input into the show. And, oh yeah, she would be getting a real salary.

"Aaron, do me a favor?" Ritz said.

"Anything, my queen," he said.

"Make sure Jamie gets to the train safely." Ritz smiled and winked at Aaron. "And make sure the two of you don't stick around too late."

"Sure thing, Ritz!" Aaron beamed.

Jamie didn't have a clue that Aaron was beaming because Ritz was looking out for him. Jamie had no idea that Aaron had a huge crush on her and gave him a swift punch to the gut.

"What are you smiling about, fool?" Jamie said.

"Nothing! Damn, girl!" said Aaron.

Ritz watched them leave the office, then she realized she was cutting it close. If she left any later, Tracee would be waiting at the airport. And Tracee hated to wait.

Her best friend was coming to town, and Ritz had insisted on picking her up. She was so excited to show Tracee her latest toy and her biggest splurge—her new Aston Martin, with the special-order champagne–peanut butter paint. She had given the detailers a lock of the weave she was sporting to match the color perfectly. The car had custom Coach leather interior—the kind you usually find in a Lexus. It was the biggest splurge Ritz had made. Chas talked her into it.

"Look, diva, you cannot be a star driving around in a what?

A Denali?" Chas said. "You better stop playing with your success like that. If you are going to be in this game, you have to have the tricks of this trade."

Ritz had to admit she was loving the new Ritz with the new toys. But she still held on to a little of the old Ritz. Inside she still remembered when she and her mother struggled. So now she made sure she paid cash for practically everything. She had great credit but she understood the business. You could be hot today and "Who's she?" the next day. And even success didn't guarantee that she would end up on top.

She remembered the stories of the famed Frankie Crocker, a radio pioneer who paved the way for many of the people who eventually made radio a career. He literally revolutionized radio with his style and voice. Radio changed forever because of Frankie, and he died in 2000 before the age of sixty, broke. There was even a rumor that there wasn't enough money left to pay for a tombstone.

Frankie Crocker was a man whose life was a flamboyant example of success. He reportedly had affairs with beautiful women like Raquel Welch, and he regularly rode though Central Park in a horse-drawn carriage. He even drove a Bentley—that was before rappers made that a standard. But he left nothing behind but debt, back taxes, and memories. Ritz would not go out like that. She wanted to own her shit outright.

So she went to the Aston Martin dealer on Eleventh Avenue in Manhattan and whipped out one hundred eighty thousand in bank checks. When she got a new piece of jewelry from Ben and Eddie at B&B Jewelers in Wayne, New Jersey, it was nothing but cash. And when she bought her furs from Pete and Bill over at Dimitrio Furs on Thirtieth Street, she paid cash. Cash was king. The only thing she owed money on was her home and her condo in Miami, which she rented out and turned a profit on every month.

Chas had turned her on to fur and she was sprung. Ritz was known for wearing fur in the summer. She even had a mink midriff custom-made. And she wished one of those PETA muthafuckers would throw some red paint on her furs. Then there would be another public scandal for the papers to write about following the ass-whipping she was prepared to throw down.

It had been just two years since Ritz's career officially took off, and she was certainly in a different place. The memories of being broke were still fresh, however. She refused to go back.

"I'll not be some broke-ass, cat-food–eating bitch," Ritz would say. "I'll at least be able to get some return on my shit if I need it."

Ritz was getting ready to finally leave the studio. She grabbed her white, calf-length fur and started gathering her effects, which she spread out on the desk everyday—cell phone, notepad and pen for notes, and a mirror (to check her face because you *never* knew who would be coming into the studio).

"Whatcha doing tonight?" Ritz said to Chas.

"I'm sticking around to make some phone calls on the station's dime," Chas said.

"That's my Mr. Frugal," Ritz teased.

"Well, if I was making your dough, I wouldn't have to worry," he said.

"You do fine," she said.

"You do *finer*," he said.

The two chuckled and Ritz gave Chas a peck on the cheek, Ritz clutching her white Gucci bag. The man at The Mall at Short Hills told her that there were only three of those bags in the entire country. It set Ritz back fifteen thousand dollars, but as Chas so aptly pointed out, she could afford it. Between her annual raises, her quarterly bonuses based on her ratings, and the appearances she was doing, Ritz was pulling down more than a million dollars a year. She was a long way from ramen noodles and crossed fingers on rent day.

Chas offered to take her bag for her as they walked out of the studio to the elevator bank.

"Yeah, right! I knew you were eyeing my bag for a minute. I got this," she said, smiling, as they headed out of the studio door.

"I just thought that with that boulder on your finger, you might not have the strength to grab your bag, too," said Chas, referring to the twelve-carat pink diamond Ritz bought herself the day before. She thought Chas would never notice. Chas had wanted to say something during the show about it but didn't get the chance.

"Have fun this weekend with Tracee," Chas said. "But don't have too much fun. You know how jealous I get when you leave me out of the rein-*girl* games."

"Boy, please!" she said. "If you're not doing anything later, drop in. I know Tracee would love to see you."

Ritz admired herself in one of the eight mirrored elevators at the elevator bank as they waited for one to open. She had her Gucci frames in her hair, holding her weave nicely in place. She had on a winter-white silk blouse under her winter-white fur, a winter-white Cavali skirt and custom-made Jimmy Choos. Ritz looked this good every day (runway ready!). But today she *felt* extra good.

Ritz knew this opportunity doing the Grammy show could lead to a regular weekly television gig if she played it right. And she planned on doing just that. Everything was all planned out—proper planning—and she was ready. Ritz Harper was exactly where she wanted to be professionally. She had money, success, and fame. She was *this close* to being the queen of all media. Ritz's personal life was as sketchy as a spiderweb, but she figured she was young enough to focus on that later. Her biological clock was about ten years from winding down. Hell, women were having their first babies for well into their forties. She would find a man and all of that, but not until she completely conquered all there was to conquer in her field.

Ritz let out a satisfied breath into the chilly February air as she rounded the corner toward her car. She could see the nose of her Aston Martin Vanquish poking out from the garage—shiny and just waiting for her. Ritz opened her pocketbook to get her parking ticket stub.

Pop! Pop! Pop! Pop!

Ritz couldn't imagine lying on the hard concrete in New York City, her life not only passing before her eyes but passing literally out of her body. Ritz Harper never imagined she would die like this.

26

Tracee made sure to bring only a carry-on bag so she wouldn't have to check any baggage and be more annoyed than she already was. The new federal rules at the airports were becoming tiresome. "Terrorism, smerrorism," she thought when she had to take off her shoes for the third time before boarding Flight 812 to Newark from Orlando. That's just why she stopped flying so much.

"Next time I'm taking Amtrak," she thought. "They don't even check your bags on the train, and I could get some sleep and not suck back all of the recycled, bad filtered air."

Tracee walked through the airy, glass-enclosed Newark Airport, passed Sbarro's and all of the lovely new shops along food row. She avoided the conveyor belts that carried the simply lazy from Point A to Point B. Since moving to Winter Garden, Tracee learned to appreciate staying fit. She tried to run three miles every day around the grounds inside her gated community. While Tracee had always had a nice shape, she was extra tight now between running and swimming in her pool.

She walked briskly past the baggage claim area out to the ground transportation area. Ritz had said she would meet her out front near the taxis, and said she had a surprise. Tracee grabbed her Motorola Razr out of her Coach bag.

The time on her phone read eight-twenty. Ritz was supposed to be there by eight-fifteen. Tracee checked to see if there were any messages on her phone. None. She was surprised that Ritz hadn't called. She always called when she was running late—which was always. Tracee decided to call to check in. Tracee was sent straight to voice-mail. She left a message.

"Hey, girl. It's me. My plane just landed and I don't have any luggage so I'm outside waiting for you."

Tracee looked up and down to see if she could spot Ritz's new Aston Martin.

"Now, what color did she say it was?" Tracee tried to remember. "Peanut butter something. To match her hair? That fool!"

There was nothing remotely close to a peanut butter–colored Aston Martin in sight.

The air felt exceptionally cold to Tracee after coming from the eighty-degree Orlando weather that she was now accustomed to. She looked down at her Nike Shox, which she had bought at the Nike outlet. She was pleased that despite being cold her feet were completely comfortable.

"Maybe she forgot the terminal," Tracee thought.

She quickly grabbed her cell phone again, remembering that she had turned it off to preserve whatever small amount of battery life she had left. Her phone beeped letting her know the SIM card had reestablished. Sure enough, there was a message.

"Hi, baby, this is Chas." Tracee smiled when she heard the familiar voice, but he didn't sound like himself. He sounded tired. "Tracee, I need you to take a cab to Sixty-eighth Street and York Avenue when you get this. Please call me when you arrive so I can meet you outside. I don't want you to be any more up—" Tracee's phone died.

She felt panic run through her body. A panic she hadn't felt since her days at the record company. What was going on and where was she meeting Chas? And why? And where was Ritz?

Tracee picked up her large Coach sack and walked to the cab stand, got in line, and waited for the next cab. Before she got in, she asked the line attendant if they accepted credit cards. Tracee almost never carried cash. And because she expected Ritz to pick her up, she didn't have a significant amount of cash on hand—at least not enough for the eighty-plus-dollar ride into Manhattan. Her grandmother's advice would have come in handy, had she heeded it.

"Baby, I don't care where you go or what you do. If you go

out, make sure you have enough cash to get home. I know you like the plastic. But cash will always be king!"

Tracee stepped into the yellow cab. It was dank and smelly in the back.

"Do you take credit cards?" Tracee asked, just to verify.

"Sure, sure!" the cab driver responded in a strong West African accent. He asked where she was headed.

Tracee gave him the address and tried not to let her imagination get the better of her. "I'll kill Ritz if she tries to have me up in some club as tired as I am."

"What did you say, ma'am?"

"Oh, nothing," Tracee said. "I was just thinking out loud. I'm really tired."

"Well, you don't look tired," the cabbie said. "I don't want you to think that I mean any harm, but you look beautiful."

"Well, thank you, sir." Tracee was drop-dead beautiful but never played the part. Most people thought her beauty started with her thousand-watt smile. Tracee was paper-bag brown with thick, naturally curly hair and beautiful almond-shaped eyes. The beauty didn't stop at her face; her body was also perfect. She could body double for Janet Jackson—the fit Janet. The body Janet had on her "All for You" concert tour. Despite her adult gifts, Tracee had a childlike way about her that everyone loved. However, the most beautiful thing about Tracee came from the inside. It was rare to be a complete beauty.

Tracee wondered why Chas had sounded so serious.

"There was truly a first time for everything," she thought as she drifted off to sleep.

"We're here, ma'am. Ma'am?"

"Oh, okay. Yes. Yes, okay," Tracee said as she quickly opened her eyes and struggled to seem alert.

Tracee handed the cab driver her platinum American Express card and tried to figure out exactly where she was. The only thing across the street was a park and this building that looked like a hospital.

What was going on?

27

After the church meeting, Pastor Edwin Lakes returned to an empty home. His wife, Patricia had taken the kids and left. She was staying with Kim, who was more than happy to squeeze the Lakes family in with her own.

Patricia had told Edwin she needed some time and space to think. He didn't argue. How could he? He had ruined her life, too. He lied to her by not telling her everything about his past. But what would he say: "Oh, yeah, by the way, before coming home to take over the ministry, I had a homosexual love affair that I really enjoyed but left because I needed to be responsible. I think about him from time to time and every now and then I even get an urge to explore that side of me again, but I pray about it and I pray about it and then I look at you and our children and those urges just go away."

Maybe he could have gotten away with that. But more than likely Patricia would have never gotten involved with him in the first place. But maybe he should have told her anyway. Maybe.

Edwin sat in the family room. It was his favorite spot in the four-thousand-square-foot home in Millburn, New Jersey. The family room was just off the kitchen, and he could eat and watch videos with his wife and kids and fall asleep on the plush sectional. He loved to cook and he loved to eat and he loved spending time with his family.

Edwin designed the home and paid extra-special attention to the family room and kitchen. He wanted that space to be almost seamless. The kitchen had a Jenn-Air stove with a built-in grill, where he loved grilling burgers and salmon steaks. There was an island in the middle of the kitchen with a warm granite top and bar stools with matching stools at the breakfast bar that separated the kitchen from the family room. He loved to gather with his wife there with four-year-old Edwin III at the table and little eighteen-month-old Ashley in her high chair as they talked over waffles and sausages.

Edwin didn't feel much like eating. And he didn't feel like going upstairs to the empty bedroom, either. So he plopped onto the sectional, grabbed the remote, and started flicking.

He sat there feeling really low. The UPN 9 News came on and Brenda Blackmon had a special report: "New York shock jock Ritz Harper has been gunned down on Park Avenue. She's in critical condition. There are no suspects. Police are investigating."

Edwin was stunned.

Brenda Blackmon kicked it to a reporter who was outside of the hospital. It seemed like a circus atmosphere. According to the reporter, they didn't know whether she had survived the shooting.

Edwin sat on his sectional and said a silent prayer for Ritz Harper. As angry as he was at Ritz and Ivan, he asked God to forgive Ivan and he prayed that Ritz would survive.

"I believe there is hope for her, Lord."

28

Delilah Summers was curled up in a California king-size bed with her Pottery Barn faux-sheepskin blanket covering her. Since she lost her job two years ago, she found it hard to get out of the house and, on most days, even her bed. Making the television millions for all of those years left Delilah with more than enough money to live for the rest of her life simply vegging out. But she wanted to get back in the game. More than anything, she wanted to get back at Ritz Harper.

It was because of that "bitch" (which was the only way Delilah would refer to Ritz now) that she had lost the job she absolutely loved. She lost her career. Delilah Summers lost her life.

"That fucking bitch!" was the constant thought that Delilah had playing over and over and over again. "She will get hers!"

Delilah actually hadn't spent the entire time in bed. She had been plotting, planning, orchestrating her next move. She was too smart and too savvy to be down forever, and she understood a few things about her business. The most important thing: Everyone can make a comeback.

They—the media and the people—loved to build you up and knock you down. On the other side of that equation: They loved to see a comeback. They loved to see Vanessa Williams lose her Miss America crown because of those *Penthouse* pictures only to come back to be a huge star in music and film. They loved to see Halle Berry get caught in a hit-and-run scandal and failed marriages only to come back and win an Oscar. They loved to see Martha Stewart become the first female billionaire in America, get caught lying to the feds, and go to jail only to come back to see her business return to its old glory.

"Delilah Summers will be back!" she told herself every day. "And Ritz Harper will have her day, too."

Revenge seemed to be the only thing keeping Delilah Summers afloat, that and a good accountant who had invested her money so wisely that she could maintain her multimillion-dollar penthouse on the Upper West Side of Manhattan without one shred of worry.

Delilah might have lost many of her so-called friends following the scandal uncovered by Ritz Harper. But no one really had any friends in her business. She did, though, have a few favors owed to her, and it was time to call them in.

Delilah had gained about fifteen pounds. She knew she would have to get off her ass and get back into the race soon.

"I'll start my diet next week," she reasoned.

Until then, her nightstand was piled high with empty Häagen-Dazs containers, empty potato chip bags, bottles of Pepsi and Arizona Iced Tea. She propped herself up on three pillows and settled in to watch the twenty-four-hour news programs on Fox, MSNBC, and CNN. She was a news junkie still and missed being at the center of it all.

"I'll be back!"

CNN had a news flash: "Radio personality Ritz Harper has been shot. It is unknown whether she has survived, but according to our sources, she was shot four times. Stay tuned for further details as we get them."

Delilah grabbed a sheet of paper from under a bottle of Pepsi on her nightstand. The paper had a list with numbers next to them. Delilah grabbed a pen and put a line through the first item on her list.

"One down, five more to go," she whispered to herself as a huge smile crossed her face.

29

The cab driver gave Tracee her card back but before he could get out to open the door for her, she was out and striding toward the hospital. The cab driver blew his horn and sped away but Tracee hadn't noticed. She looked up and down the street hoping to see Ritz or Chas, but all she saw were a lot of television trucks and what looked like paparazzi huddled around the emergency room entrance. Tracee felt uncontrollable heat rising from her neck. She knew the evening would not end without a migraine.

Tracee walked past the press and into the hospital, straight to the security station. She didn't know what to say or what to ask the hospital security. She was lost.

"Can I help you?" the attendant asked.

Tracee's voice cracked but she was able to finally get the words out. "I don't know. I'm looking for a friend. I'm not sure what he's wearing but he's a tall black man and, and . . ."

Tracee felt crazy. This was not at all what she planned for this trip.

"Tracee! Tracee!" It was Chas.

"What's going on?!"

"Ritz. She's been shot. I don't know how many times. I don't know what her status is. I don't know anything really. Now you know as much as I do."

"Oh my God! Oh my God! No!" Tracee was practically screaming at the top of her lungs. Chas pulled her into his arms and she cried uncontrollably. Chas rested his chin on the top of her head, holding her tight for his own comfort as well as hers.

A redheaded doctor walked out of ER and over to the nurses' station. The emergency room nurse pointed to Chas, and Chas didn't wait for an invitation to walk over. Tracee was right beside him holding him hard.

"Are you the brother of Jane Doe?"

Ritz was originally listed as a Jane Doe because she had no identification on her when she arrived in the ambulance. The media knew she was Ritz Harper because an eyewitness called it in. But she had not been officially identified. Her fifteen-thousand-dollar bag had been stolen along with her Gucci frames and her new diamond ring.

"Jane Doe?"

"Yes. The young woman arrived here with no identification and just the clothes on her back."

"Her name is Ritz Harper. Ritz Harper," Chas said.

"It would help if I can ask you about her medical history so we can know if there are any precautions we should take or if there are any allergies to any medication," said the doctor. "Right now I can tell you that she is in critical condition. She was shot three times—once in the shoulder, once in the chest, which punctured a lung, and the last bullet passed through her side. Right now the only thing we can do is wait and pray."

Tracee began to cry again and ask why.

"Can we see her?" Chas asked.

The doctor led Tracee and Chas to the ICU. They were able to stand outside the glass and look at her.

"Why is her head bandaged?" Tracee managed to get out between sniffles.

"She seems to have suffered a concussion and a huge gash when her head hit the concrete.

Ritz looked not only like had she been shot but she also resembled Mike Tyson after his fight with Lennox Lewis. Her eyes were swollen closed and tubes seemed to be coming from every part of her body.

Tracee's stomach lurched; she had to leave immediately. Chas turned to the doctor and said they would be back.

Tracee and Chas went to the family lounge. Tracee needed to sit before she fell. A migraine had started to work its way through her head, shredding her frayed nerves to pieces.

"Chas, who could have done this?"

"Tracee, take your pick on that one," he said. "I don't even know where to begin."

"I can't believe this!" she said. "I never thought people would take what Ritz does for more than entertainment."

"Tracee, what Ritz says on the radio is as serious as the stuff that killed Tupac and Biggie," Chas said.

"Oh, no!" Tracee said. "Did you call Ritz's aunt and uncle?"

"I don't even have a number for them."

"I'll call them. I just hope that they get the news from me and not from the television."

The doctor told Chas and Tracee that there wasn't much for them to do at the hospital, and he advised them to go home. But Tracee wasn't leaving Ritz. She and Chas went outside to get some fresh air and were met by a throng of reporters from every major newspaper, magazine, supermarket tabloid, and television news outlet.

With the lack of concrete news, it was turning into a media feeding frenzy. Everyone was trying to be the first with the next update.

"Excuse me! Did you say her parents are on vacation?" said one NY-1 reporter who had managed to sneak inside and was standing behind Tracee and Chas the whole time, eavesdropping. It took every ounce of strength for Tracee not to slap the shit out of her.

Seeing Tracee's anger, the reporter moved away without asking another question. Chas grabbed Tracee's arm and ushered her back to the lounge area.

As they sat waiting, a tall, handsome man in a nicely fitted suit walked over to them with authority. "You two come with me."

"Who are you?" Tracee asked, worried.

"Please, ma'am, I'll tell you everything, just come with me."

Detective Tom Pelov walked briskly down the corridor with Chas and Tracee. They went through two large white doors. Beyond the door there was little movement except for the occasional passing of a nurse. Pelov stopped and introduced himself.

"My name is Detective Pelov. I'm with homicide, and I have been assigned to this case."

Tracee screamed.

ABOUT THE AUTHORS

☆ ★ ☆

WENDY WILLIAMS, a top-rated syndicated radio host, has published two *New York Times* bestsellers—*Wendy's Got the Heat* and *The Wendy Williams Experience*. In addition to her books and radio show, she also hosts a television show on VH1. Wendy lives in New Jersey with her husband, Kevin, and their son. This is her debut novel.

KAREN HUNTER, a Pulitzer Prize–winning editorial writer, has coauthored ten books, including *New York Times* bestsellers *On the Down Low*, *Wendy's Got the Heat*, *The Wendy Williams Experience*, *I Make My Own Rules*, and *Ladies First*. Karen hosts a morning show on WWRL (1600 AM) in New York and is an assistant professor in the Department of Film and Media Studies at Hunter College. This is her first novel.